LAWMAN'S DUTY

Center Point
Large Print

Also by James Clay and available from Center Point Large Print:

Devil's Due
Satan's Guns
The Justice Rider
Stalking the Dragon
Serpent's Bite
Gunfighter's Revenge
Deadly Betrayal

LAWMAN'S DUTY

A RANCE DEHNER WESTERN

JAMES CLAY

CENTER POINT LARGE PRINT
THORNDIKE, MAINE

This Center Point Large Print edition
is published in the year 2025 by arrangement with
the author.

Copyright © 2024 by James Clay.

All rights reserved.

The text of this Large Print edition is unabridged.
In other aspects, this book may vary
from the original edition.
Printed in the United States of America
on permanent paper sourced using
environmentally responsible foresting methods.
Set in 16-point Times New Roman type.

ISBN: 979-8-89164-515-8

The Library of Congress has cataloged this record
under Library of Congress Control Number: 2024951731

LAWMAN'S DUTY

CHAPTER ONE

Heat lightning flashed across Travis, Arizona, throwing a short metallic glow over the bat wings of the Dusty Trail Saloon. The handful of men leaning against the bar looked around in mild surprise. The smudgy lamps fastened on the wall near the bar provided only a weak kerosene yellow. Nature had exposed the saloon's belief that men didn't need light to get drunk.

Not that anyone much cared. At ten o'clock on a Monday night the place was less than half full. Most of the men there were hunched over drinks, trying to forget they had nothing better to do and never would.

The back wall of the saloon was a different universe. The lighting was good, and Luther Darcel was enjoying his weekly poker game with the town's leading citizens. Being the richest man of the group, Luther could dictate the night of their weekly competition. The rancher favored Monday. His selection reflected his power. Let the weaklings cling to Friday and Saturday nights. He would decide when the important citizens of Travis would gamble into the wee hours.

Nobody noticed the strange apparition that entered quietly through the bat wings. The woman was wearing a long raincoat, which was hardly necessary on the hot, sultry night. She was barefoot and staggering slightly. Her hands were emaciated to the point of looking like claws.

"Luther . . . Darcel!" the name screeched across the saloon.

Darcel looked up from his cards. His body twitched and his eyes widened. The hunched shadow limped from the partial darkness which blanketed the bar area and advanced toward the rancher.

Darcel rose to his feet and leaned forward. The apparition that approached him was one of impending death. Skin that looked like worn parchment covered a pale, bony face. Her body trembled as if it could barely hold up under the burden of walking. Wires of red hair zigged without purpose across her head.

Only the woman's eyes contained life. They blazed with a feverish intensity from dark sockets. "Remember me, Luther?"

The rancher replied in a soft whisper. "My God . . . you're . . . Penny."

The woman replied with a coarse laugh. "Yes! Penny Jarrett! Ya used to joke and call me Penny's Worth when ya visited me. When I gave birth to our son, Thad."

"I don't know what you're talkin' about."

The atmosphere in the Dusty Trail had been tense since Penny screamed the rancher's name. Now the tension rose by several notches. Despite his words, the tone of Darcel's voice signaled he knew exactly what the woman was talking about.

Keeping her eyes on Luther Darcel, Penny shouted to the bartender. "Ike, ya ever wonder how Sadie Morgan was able to give up a room in her boarding house to raise a kid 'til he turned fourteen?"

Ike wanted no part in whatever it was that Penny was doing. "Never gave it no thought."

"Because Luther Darcel was paying her. After Sadie died, he gave Thad a job on his ranch. A real charitable man, Luther Darcel. Well, now my boy is twenty-one . . ."

Penny's voice became a wheeze. She bent over and coughed uncontrollably as a young man wearing a black broadcloth coat hurried into the saloon.

One of the men at the bar shouted, "Here to save souls, Preacher?" The tinkle of laughter that followed was solely to relieve tension.

Reverend Bo Jefferson paid no heed to the scoffer. He ran to Penny Jarrett and caught her by both arms as she began to collapse.

Jefferson had only been in Travis for a few months. Luther Darcel, who knew everything about the town, was aware that the preacher had recently graduated from a school in the East. He might be wet behind the ears, but he was a man to be taken seriously. Jefferson had a pistol strapped to his waist and knew how to use it.

The rancher's voice was amicable. "Looks like you're takin' care of the sick tonight, Bo."

Jefferson spoke reassuringly to Penny, then turned to Darcel. "Afraid I'm not doing a very good job. Penny is staying at the surgery in Doctor Colbert's house. Reuben had to leave on a call, asked me to look in on her from time to time. On my second visit she was gone."

Penny could no longer stand without help, but her eyes maintained their ferocious burn. Her voice gained new strength as she shouted at the rancher. "You treat Thad Jarrett fair! Treat him like your son, that's what he is!"

The parson cautiously turned the woman around and began to walk her toward the batwings. Luther Darcel felt he had to say something. "Need any help, Bo?"

To Darcel's relief, Jefferson answered with a "No thanks." But was there something edgy about the preacher's voice? Did Bo Jefferson at least half believe what the woman had just shouted?

One of the customers at the bar yelled out, "No need ta take Penny back to Doc's, Sky Pilot, jus' drop her in an alley somewhere. The undertaker can scoop her up and bury her tomorra' mornin'."

"Shut up, Zeke," Darcel ordered.

A blond-haired man of twenty-three stepped away from the bar and looked at his father. "No need ta git all fussed, Pa. I was jus' funnin' the sky pilot."

As the pastor guided Penny through the bat wings, Luther Darcel decided to treat the incident as a joke. He raised his voice in a light hearted manner. "Poor Penny, sickness has made the ol' gal crazy. Sure is sad to see. I think we all need a drink to cheer us up. I'm buyin'!"

Darcel made a quick hand gesture signaling that the card game was done. The three other men at the table said nothing.

The rancher headed for the bar, where he slapped backs and swapped stories as if he were running for office. After more than thirty minutes of forced jolliness, he pulled Zeke aside.

"We gotta head back to the ranch, pronto."

Zeke had completely accepted the jolly act as the real thing. "Why, Pa? Things is swell here."

The rancher angrily whispered to his son, "Do what I tell ya!" Then he once again became the jovial host as he shouted, "Make sure the boys are kept happy, Ike. Put the cost on me!"

Luther Darcel pushed his son through the bat wings and followed after him.

Thad Jarrett stopped before leaving the large bunkhouse. He quickly glanced around at the twenty-two men who were there. Some were playing cards; others were jawing with each other. A few were reading newspapers or magazines, and one was reading a book. The ramrod stepped outside. He had already checked on the four ranch hands doing first watch on the herd. Thad felt confident that all was well. He could leave for a few hours.

He was heading for the stable of the Big D Ranch when he saw Luther Darcel and his son Zeke riding toward him. Thad obligingly stopped and waited for the two riders. After all, Luther Darcel, the owner of the ranch, was his boss. There was an understanding that Zeke would also be treated as a boss, although any orders he gave were to be double checked with his father.

Both riders pulled up their horses on either side of Thad. "Where do you think you're goin'?"

Thad was surprised by the harshness of the ranch owner's voice. He kept his own voice amicable. "Jus' riding into town to check on my mother, Mr. Darcel. She's powerful sick, the doctor says—"

"Your ma is dead," Luther Darcel thought he was probably telling the truth. "And ya ain't goin' inta town. Not for a long time."

Thad was shocked. "How'd you know—"

"Never mind, get back to the bunkhouse, ya gotta be up early."

"No, Mr. Darcel. I've never bucked you before, but I'm riding into town to see what's happened to my mother."

Luther Darcel closed his eyes as he nodded twice to Zeke. Thad was still facing the ranch owner as Zeke drew his pistol and slammed it against the ramrod's head. Thad yelled in pain as he hit the ground. Zeke laughed as he slid off his horse and once again hammered Thad's skull.

"Woohoo!" Zeke proclaimed joyfully. "Thad looks like he'll sleep all week."

"Shut up," the ranch owner ordered his son for the second time that night. "Get Thad's horse saddled and ready. I'll be right back." He turned his horse and spurred it into a gallop toward the ranch house.

Contrary to Zeke's assertion, Thad Jarrett was not totally unconscious. But Jarrett's sight was blurry, and he knew he couldn't stand up. The young man caressed his side. His gun still rested in his holster. He decided to leave it there.

The ramrod vaguely wondered if he was having a nightmare. Nothing made sense. Why had he been assaulted?

What little thinking Thad was capable of was confused even more by Luther Darcel. The ranch owner suddenly crouched over Thad, speaking in a soft voice. "Can you hear me okay, boy?"

"Yes . . . why . . ."

"Never mind that now. Try drinking this." He held a canteen to Thad's lips. The young man drank and felt better. Maybe he misunderstood what had happened to him. Maybe an accident . . .

Zeke walked Thad's horse out of the stable. "This here is a fine animal, Pa. Let's give Jarrett another one and keep—"

"The appaloosa belongs ta Thad," Zeke's father shot back. "I gave it ta him myself."

The rancher was still crouched over his ramrod. "Can ya stand up, boy?"

"Guess so." With Luther holding on to one of his arms, Thad rose to his feet.

But a wave of nausea came over Jarrett. He broke away from the ranch owner, took several steps from his boss and vomited.

"I'm sorry, Sir."

Luther's voice remained soft. "Nothin' to be sorry about. Ya jus' clear your head. Then we're takin' a ride."

Thad Jarrett was incapable of asking questions about the ride. He surprised himself by mounting the appaloosa without help. Shortly after the three men rode off from the ranch, Thad began to doze in the saddle.

"Thad!" The young man was awakened by his boss' voice. He had no idea how much time had passed.

"Yes . . . Mr. Darcel?"

"Get off your horse," Darcel had dismounted and was standing beside the appaloosa. "Somethin' I gotta tell ya."

As Thad dismounted, he realized his head had been bandaged. Luther Darcel must have done it before giving him the water. "Guess I passed out for a spell after all," he whispered.

With uncertain steps, Thad Jarrett stumbled

toward a large cottonwood and leaned against it, taking in his surroundings. The young man realized he was in one of his favorite spots. A place he visited to relax.

The ranch owner spoke in a nervous, overly friendly manner as he pointed at the nearby stream. "You and me had some good times fishin' here, didn't we?"

Thad felt increasingly edgy. His world had suddenly turned bizarre. Still, he managed to respond politely. "Yes Sir, we did."

"I sure was happy on those days," Luther looked at the stream, then spoke to the ground. "You're my son, my flesh and blood. But nobody can find out. Penny's your ma and ya know, Penny..."

"Yes, I know," even in his weakened state, anger tinged Thad's voice.

"Penny stormed inta The Dusty Trail tonight, told ever'one there I was your pa," Luther Darcel still couldn't look at Thad. "Some may have believed her. The way things stand, they'll keep quiet. But ya look like me, boy. If ya go inta town, folks will start talkin', 'Luther Darcel had a son by that whore, Penny Jarrett.'"

Luther kicked at the ground viciously. "I had this notion that maybe ya could jus' stay on the ranch, never go inta Travis. Guess that was a fool idea."

"Yes," the young man responded. "It was foolish."

Still without looking at his injured son, the ranch owner turned and walked toward the horses. As Luther quickly opened one of his saddle bags, Zeke spoke in an ingratiating manner, desperate for his father's attention. "Pa, I was thinkin' maybe . . ."

Luther abruptly returned to the cottonwood. He didn't care what Zeke was thinking.

He approached Thad with both hands stretched out, carrying a small canvas sack. "This here bag has a lotta money, boy. Some of it gold coins, some banknotes. Ride far away from here. Buy some land. Start over."

"I don't want your money."

Luther Darcel's voice became pleading. "Take the money, Thad! Ya deserve it! I'm sa proud of ya. I'd like for the whole damn world ta know you're my boy, but . . ."

The rancher once again faced the ground. The motion couldn't hide his tears. His voice was broken and high pitched. "I can't have people laughin' at me. Makin' jokes behind my back. I worked hard ta build the Big D, ta be a man folks respected. All that would be lost when it got out I had me a son by a whore." He lifted his face and looked directly at Thad. "Do ya understand?"

Thad felt a strange sympathy for the man standing in front of him. "Yes Sir, I think I understand."

Still facing his injured son, Luther Darcel

barked a sound of both laughter and despair. "Why don't ya call me Pa? Jus' this once."

Thad hesitated, then spoke quietly. "Sure . . . Pa. I'll go away. Thanks for letting me work at the ranch, Sir . . . I mean . . . Pa."

The rancher gave a wide smile which bordered on madness. He nodded his head and laid the canvas sack near his son's feet.

"I wish things coulda' been different," those words collided into mush as the older Darcel ran back to his horse. He mounted and rode off quickly, not even acknowledging Zeke's presence. Confusion covered Zeke's face as he turned to face his half-brother, then mounted and rode after his father.

Thad continued to lean against the tree as a myriad of emotions ran through him. After a few minutes, the pain in his head subsided a bit. "No sense in staying here," he slapped the cottonwood as if saying goodbye to a friend.

Walking toward his horse, he stepped on the canvas bag. He cautiously stooped down and picked it up. Without opening it, he placed the item in one of his saddle bags. Thad Jarrett then slowly mounted his appaloosa and patted the animal's neck. "You must have thought that would take me till sunup."

Sunup was still hours away as Thad Jarrett rode into Travis. He pulled up in front of the home and office of Dr. Reuben Colbert. As he stepped into the house, he heard familiar voices coming from the surgery.

"Should we take her to the undertaker?" Bo Jefferson was speaking.

"No. She can stay here until morning," Dr. Colbert replied. "I'll send someone out to the Big D to let Thad know his mother has passed."

Jarrett quietly stepped out of the house and mounted his horse. Another wave of nausea assaulted him. As the world came back into focus, he whispered to the appaloosa, "I have a promise to keep to Mr. Darcel. We're leaving this place. But I gotta feeling we're coming back."

As the young man rode out of town, the sky burst with a wave of lightning. For a moment, Thad took it as a premonition of brutality and death.

CHAPTER TWO

Three Years Later

At well past nine in the morning, the one restaurant in Snake Creek, Arizona buzzed with conversation and laughter. Outside Flint's Fine Foods, children played in the street. The settlement's only saloon, the Red Dog, had been open all night and was still doing big business.

The community lacked a hotel, so people were camped out at Snake Creek's edges. Some of the visitors were clapping their hands and singing.

Excitement and joy were everywhere. After all, in a little more than an hour, people would be able to watch, at no expense, one man kill another.

Pastor Bo Jefferson noted the festive atmosphere as he rode his black into town. He turned the animal into Ollie's Livery. He was greeted by the owner. "Mornin', Preacher."

"Good morning, Ollie," Bo proclaimed as he dismounted. "Looks like I'm not the only person from Travis to be visiting Snake Creek today."

"Folks is comin' from all over," Ollie declared, waving both arms. He was a short, portly man, who, given his business, always looked surprisingly clean.

"Please give Noah the works," Bo requested as he patted his horse. "I got started a bit late this morning. He's been ridden hard for the last hour or so."

"Sure thing. Youse is lucky, Preacher. I only got me one stall left. Last night, I made some extra money from people wantin' to sleep in my hayloft. Nothin' like a gunfight between two real poorfessionals to git folks stirred up."

Bo's face turned grim. "As I understand it, the trouble started when the son of a wealthy rancher killed the son of the owner of the Red Dog."

"Yep," Ollie agreed. "The boy who got hisself shot was tendin' bar. Frank, he's the rancher's boy, says the barkeep cheated him. Don't know if that's true."

The pastor nodded his head. "Snake Creek doesn't have law. So, the bar owner hired Music Matt McCall to kill Frank."

"Yep," Ollie repeated. "And the rancher hired Thad Jarrett to kill Matt McCall. Say, didn't youse once know Thad?"

"Yes."

"Folks say he's fast, but not as fast as McCall. Guess you're here to find out?"

Bo Jefferson hid his irritation with the question. "No. After the fight's over, I want to talk with Thad."

Ollie bellowed a laugh. "Youse sound mighty con-fee-dent 'bout the outcome!"

Jefferson didn't respond to the livery owner's remark. In truth, he had no idea how the fight would come out. He settled for paying Ollie in advance, then nodded good-bye.

"Hold on," Ollie pointed at the Winchester in the scabbard of the pastor's saddle. "That's a fine gun. Better take it with you. A lot of strangers will be in and out of this here place today. Some might have sticky fingers."

Bo felt embarrassed about his earlier irritation with the livery owner. He smiled a "thanks" at the man and retrieved the rifle.

Cradling the Winchester as if he were starting out on a hunting trip, Bo paused then asked, "Do you know when Matt McCall started calling himself Music Matt McCall?"

Ollie scratched the top of his head. "I think he started the singin' stuff a little over a year back. Began wearin' a flashy red string tie 'bout the same time. Some folks say an Eastern writer gave Matt the notions, figurin' it would put a shine on his reputation. Make him different from the other gunneys. Guess that could be why he started doin' it."

"Guess it could be," Bo agreed, but he sounded uncertain.

Walking from the livery toward what passed as the center of Snake Creek, Jefferson noted the usual cones of dust drifting about like helpless drunks. Boardwalks were still in the future for the settlement. Snake Creek existed only because of cattle ranches. The settlement was much more attuned to the needs of cows than those of people.

Several citizens of Snake Creek rode into Travis every Sunday to attend church. Jefferson exchanged quick "hellos" with a few familiar faces. One parishioner grabbed the pastor by his arm. "Take cover Preacher, the shootin' is gonna be at ten in front of the Red Dog. That's only a few minutes from now."

Jefferson thanked the man but didn't take his advice. The pastor's mind was frantically juggling thoughts. So many things about this gunfight were, well, odd. The time, to begin with: ten in the morning, a strange hour for a gunfight.

"But when is a good time for a gunfight?" Bo heard his own voice ask.

The pastor was now standing directly across the dirt street from the Red Dog Saloon. He took a few steps leftward to where he was under the overhang of a gun shop. The place appeared empty. No surprise. Shad's Gun Shop boasted only one small window. Shad, like all the other spectators, was now someplace with a large window and a good view.

Jefferson squinted as he looked across the street at the Red Dog. The sun's hot spears were almost blinding.

A jittery silence cloaked the settlement. A

deep baritone voice singing a hymn suddenly dominated the surroundings.

"When the trumpet of the Lord shall sound and time shall be no more, and the morning breaks eternal bright and fair . . ."

A tall, angular shadow was highlighted in the bright sun as it walked through the unsettled dust. Music Matt McCall's voice seemed to become louder as he approached the Red Dog. Thad Jarrett stepped into the sunlight from an alley just a few yards up from where Bo was standing. Thad walked to the center of the street where he directly faced the approaching gunman.

Jarrett's back was to the pastor. Thad was standing straight and still, assessing his opponent.

McCall stopped singing but his voice still boomed. "Brother, I am here to bring justice to this lawless settlement. I urge you to leave now and allow me to avenge a murder."

"You know . . ." Thad Jarrett had just started to reply when Jefferson spotted a squirming motion on the roof of the Red Dog. Things began to make sense. The owner of the saloon had hired Matt McCall. McCall's singing had focused all attention on himself. The sun made it hard to spot anything on the Red Dog's roof.

Jefferson levered his Winchester as McCall went for his gun. An explosion of gunfire followed along with searing screams of pain. A body tumbled off the Red Dog's roof and hit the

23

ground. Matt McCall staggered backwards, one bullet from Jarrett's gun burning in his side.

McCall viewed the body of his accomplice, then looked at Thad Jarrett in amazement, as if wondering how Jarrett wised up to the trick.

"Drop your gun, McCall," Jarrett yelled, his smoking gun pointed directly at his opponent.

Matt McCall glanced at the unfired weapon in his hand. Surrender would mean a lifetime of torment. The great Music Matt McCall was nothing but a shoddy travelling show trickster, dependent on a hidden gunney to kill his opponents. People would laugh at him. He couldn't walk into a saloon without being mocked.

"Hell would be better." McCall whispered to himself.

McCall's sight was becoming blurry. His ears buzzed but he could still hear a threatening voice. "Drop the gun, last chance."

A desperate notion flamed in McCall's mind as his life seeped away. In a hoarse but still strong voice he shouted, "Matt McCall is visitin' his pal the devil for a while. But he ain't defeated. I'll be back and kill ya, Jarrett. Here's something to help ya remember me . . ."

The bleeding gunman raised his weapon. A second bullet ripped into his chest and sent him sprawling onto the ground. He only squirmed for a few seconds.

Gun in hand, Jarrett slowly approached the two

bodies lying in front of him. Satisfied both men were dead, he holstered his Colt and turned to face the man now standing behind him.

"Good morning, Preacher, long time no see." He pointed to the corpse that had been shot off the Red Dog roof. "Thanks for the help. Let me buy you a cup of coffee."

CHAPTER THREE

A crowd gathered outside Flint's Fine Foods, staring through the window at the two men dining inside. One boy almost had his face pressed against the glass. "Pa, ain't that the preacher sittin' at the table with Thad Jarrett?"

"Yep."

"Think mebbe we kin go to church this Sunday? Bet the preacher will jaw some 'bout Thad."

Inside the restaurant, Charlie Flint was bringing his two customers cups of coffee. "Like anything to eat, gents? It's all on the house."

"Steak and eggs for both of us," Thad ordered. "I'll pay."

Charlie hesitated, wondering whether to press his declaration about everything being on the house. Deciding against it, he headed for the kitchen.

"Killing a man makes me hungry," Jarrett told his companion.

Bo wasn't certain if Thad Jarrett was joking. He noted the changes in the young man who had left Travis three years ago. He had put on several pounds, none of it fat. His face remained unlined, but the boyish enthusiasm had vanished from his eyes.

A trace of that boyishness remained in Jarrett's

voice. "Tell me, Preacher, how'd you know about McCall having an accomplice?"

"I didn't know. I just pieced things together."

"What do you mean?"

"You're not going to like part of what I say."

Jarrett laughed good naturedly. "Go ahead. I won't shoot you."

"Reputation is often a few steps behind reality," Jefferson explained. "McCall used to get close to a thousand dollars for a job. You've seen the Red Dog Saloon. The owner probably couldn't pay more than a couple hundred dollars."

Thad nodded his head. "The rancher paid me three hundred."

Bo continued. "McCall began the singing and red tie routine about a year ago. My guess goes that he injured his arm. He couldn't draw all that fast anymore. So, he got an accomplice and only took on jobs where he could dictate terms. He would set a time and location where the sun or something else would hide his accomplice."

"The singing and sometimes the red tie would keep the attention on him."

"Yep." Jefferson affirmed. "If he had succeeded, he probably would have ambushed the rancher's son."

A look of genuine sympathy creased Jarrett's face. "I almost feel sorry for the jasper. Can you imagine how important his reputation was to Matt McCall? With all the money he made, he could have vanished into Mexico and lived well. But no, he couldn't give up being a fast gun. Even if it meant only showing off in small holes like Snake Creek where people would just bury his victims without looking over the wounds."

"Yes," Jefferson replied. "In my line of work, I deal a lot with the follies of pride. I'm here to rescue you from all that."

Both men stopped talking as Charlie arrived carrying a tray of food and eating utensils. After carefully arranging plates and cutlery on the table, he hurried off and returned with a coffee pot. He made sure both of his customers had full cups, then nervously asked, "Anything more I can do for you gents?"

"No thanks," Thad answered.

Charlie looked at the crowd gathered outside the window. He made an elaborate nod as if acknowledging applause, then hurried off.

After cutting his steak, chewing down, and swallowing a tough piece of meat, Thad Jarrett resumed the conversation. "I appreciate you saving my life, Preacher. But my soul is a different matter. Be obliged if you'd leave it alone."

"I wasn't talking about your soul. I have a worldly offer to make."

"I don't follow you."

"I have been authorized by the city council of Travis to offer you the job of sheriff."

Thad took a long drink of coffee. A cautious, quizzical expression blanketed his face as he placed the cup back on the table. "What's up? Travis has a sheriff, Quaid Markham. Hear he's real good at keeping law and order."

"Too good."

Thad moved his food about on the plate. "You need to explain some."

"When he took the badge, Markham started demanding the business establishments give him what he wanted—free. I'm not talking about a few drinks on the house. Quaid Markham gets free haircuts, ammunition from the gun shop, food from the restaurants, all the liquor he can put down and anything he wants from the general store."

The gunfighter shrugged his shoulders. "Sounds like the business folks don't mind going along."

"They've been going along for close to two years: a big mistake."

Something fired in Thad's eyes. "Markham is starting to demand protection money?"

"Yep. Abe Kibler refused to pay Markham the five dollars a month he demanded to keep the general store protected." Bo's voice layered heavy sarcasm over "protected," then the pastor continued. "Last week, someone broke into the store from a back door while Abe was doing his inventory. Abe ended up on the floor with a bleeding skull. He's recovered and still refuses to pay the money."

"Abe is a good man," Thad whispered, partially to himself. "Always treated my mother with respect. Not all the merchants did. Does Quaid Markham work alone?"

"No, he has a deputy, a thug named Hoke."

Thad glanced at the window and the crowd who were staring at him. He quickly looked away. "I heard Mr. Darcel died, over a year ago."

"Yes. Doctor Colbert said it was a heart attack."

"Who heads up the town council now?"

"Your half-brother."

"Zeke Darcel's agreeable to the notion of me packing a star in Travis?!"

A new intensity came into the pastor's voice. "Zeke is scared. So is most of the town. Quaid Markham is talking about hiring new deputies. In other words, he's going to have a team of hardcases behind him."

"He'll rule, and pity anyone who bucks him," Thad supplied.

"Exactly."

"Are you on the town council?"

"No. They only sent me—"

Thad finished the pastor's remark. "Because you were decent to my mother in the last couple months of her life, and they reckoned I'd be grateful. Tell them they're right about that. Then tell them I don't think their offer is worth a thimble full of warm spit."

Jarrett paused. When he spoke again his voice

became louder. "I just made three hundred dollars. It would take me almost a year of handling gunslicks, drunken cowboys and worst of all, a passel of fools who laugh at me behind my back because . . . hell . . . tell them whatever you want, but Zeke and his pals will have to find someone else to tame their rotten town."

Bo quietly replied. "The town isn't rotten. There are plenty of good people there, like Abe Kibler. People who need your help."

Thad inhaled deeply, looked at the ceiling and said nothing.

Bo Jefferson was burrowing deep. He had known the Thad Jarrett of three years ago. That man's soul could not have been altered completely.

"What do you think really happened here in Snake Creek?"

"When you're talking to me, you need to be plain as paint, Preacher."

"The owner of the Red Dog claimed the son of a rancher murdered his boy. The rancher says otherwise. Who do you think was right?"

Jarrett shrugged. "I don't know. What difference does it make?"

Now it was the Bo's turn to raise his voice. "Two men were killed here this morning, that's why it should make a difference to you."

Jarrett's eyes wouldn't meet those of his companion. He started to reach into his shirt pocket for a tobacco pouch. "Listen . . ."

Jefferson sprang up and leaned over the table. "No, you listen. You're entering hell on earth. You're embarking on a life where you kill for the highest bidder. How many innocents will you send to an early grave? God gave you a gift. You're a warrior. You must use that gift the way God intended!"

Bo Jefferson remained on his feet, staring harshly at the gunfighter. After what seemed an eternity to Thad Jarrett, Jefferson sat down.

Jarrett inhaled deeply once again. "I never walked through a church door, but my mother did. She told me you preached something powerful. Guess you just proved her right."

Bo nodded an acknowledgement but said nothing. The harshness in his face was diminishing.

Thad once again began to reach for his tobacco. "Mind if I have a smoke?"

"Not at all," came the polite, cheerful reply.

Both men laughed as Thad built a Bull Durham cigarette. The tension Jefferson had created with his strong words dropped down several notches.

After lighting the smoke, the gunfighter's demeanor became serious. "How fast is Quaid Markham?"

Bo's response was also serious. He had been observing the situation. "Markham is not as fast as most folks in Travis think. He's had no serious competition, just kids trying to build a reputation. Quaid Markham is a brutal man but he's a mediocre gunfighter. I think he'll back down when you tell him you're moving him out of the sheriff's office. But if not, you can take him."

"How about the deputy . . . Hoke?"

"I can handle Hoke."

The gunfighter gave his companion a crooked smile. "I'll bet you can at that."

Thad remembered leaving Travis three years before. The notion that he would return had been strong then and now it was once again pulling at him. "Travis, Arizona is a far stretch from Heaven, but I reckon for me, it's home. Guess we'll be making dust for Travis. But first, let's finish our meal. Like I said, killing a man makes me hungry."

Thad Jarrett laughed as he fiddled with his cigarette. "I may be getting hungry again later on in the day."

CHAPTER FOUR

As Thad Jarrett and Bo Jefferson rode onto the Big D, the gunfighter felt more nervous than when he had faced Matt McCall a few hours before. There were a lot of unfamiliar faces scattered about the ranch. Ranch hands were a restless lot: men who dreamed of the riches and pretty women awaiting them over the next hill.

But several of the men engaged in chores around the ranch were ones that, only three years before, Thad had bossed when he was foreman of the Big D. Those men ran toward him with looks of reverence and an anxious satisfaction. Now, the tales they had told to the newcomers could be proved right. They had worked for Thad Jarrett, the famous gunfighter.

Eight men were trailing behind Thad and Bo as they tied up their horses at the rail in front of the sprawling ranch house. "Howdy, gents!" Thad declared in a friendly manner as he and the pastor dismounted.

The group responded with "howdies" shouted at a variety of levels. A hefty man, slightly below average height, broke from the group and approached Jarrett. "I hope ya ain't here ta take your ole job back," he said good naturedly. "I sure admire the extra two dollars I git ever' month."

"Whit Evans!" Jarrett's pleasure was genuine as he shook hands with a friend from his past. "So Luther Darcel had the good sense to make you the ramrod?"

"Yep." Whit paused, unsure of whether to say what was on his mind. "Ya know, Mr. Darcel never tole us why ya left."

Thad side stepped the implied question. "Sorry to hear Luther Darcel died. How's his son treating you?"

Whit quickly eyed the men surrounding him, then replied cautiously, "Fine, jus' fine."

Bo Jefferson sensed a need to jump into the conversation. "We've dropped by to see Zeke, is he in the house?"

"Nope," Whit answered. "He's seein' ta things in the stable."

Whit's voice took on a forced quality, as if the notion of Zeke Darcel "seein' ta things" was nonsense. For the next few minutes, Bo Jefferson took charge of the talk, ensuring that each man got a chance to exchange a few words with the famous gunfighter. Thad was grateful for the intervention. He couldn't remember the names of all the gathered ranch hands. The pastor knew each one.

Walking to the stable, Jarrett took in the surroundings. "From what I can tell, the Big D is prospering."

Jefferson responded with a sigh. "If there was

any justice, this place would be called the Big E. Whit Evans is the one who keeps it prosperous. Of course, we don't live in a world where justice comes naturally. In this world we need—"

The pastor abruptly cut himself off. "Sorry. I sometimes forget that Sunday morning is when I deliver a sermon."

As the two men neared the stable, they could hear an angry shout coming from inside. "The way the tack was hung up was all wrong!"

The reply was soft and could barely be heard. "Yes, Mr. Darcel."

"Don't let it happen again!"

"Yes, sir."

Zeke Darcel stormed angrily out of the stable, then came to an immediate stop. What was reflected on his face as he beheld his half-brother? Was it fear, hatred, envy . . . maybe it was all three, Thad couldn't be sure.

Zeke leaned backwards for a moment as if avoiding a punch, then spoke to Jefferson. "I see you carried out your assignment."

Thad extended his right hand. "Good to see you again, Zeke." The words sounded absurd to Jarrett, but he still thought them necessary. His half-brother needed to know that Thad Jarrett had no interest in avenging the past.

"I now head up the town council of Travis," Zeke proclaimed as the two men shook hands.

"That's what the preacher told me."

"You are here, that means you have accepted the position we offered you." Zeke sounded nervous as he tried to sound business-like.

To his own surprise, Jarrett felt sympathy for his half-brother. Zeke was only two years older than Thad but at twenty-six his midriff was already bulging over his belt. He was dressed like a banker, not a rancher.

Thad understood the fine duds. Zeke Darcel had inherited wealth and importance and didn't know how to handle either one. Others mocked Zeke behind his back, and he knew it. Thus, he felt a need to constantly assert his own high rank.

"We'll ride into Travis immediately," Zeke Darcel snapped the order. "Upon arrival, I'll call an emergency meeting of the town council. You are required to formally accept their offer and be sworn in before you can assume your responsibilities."

Bo Jefferson cringed. Thad Jarrett smiled kindly.

"Fine," the soon to be sheriff said.

The town council consisted of four men, including Zeke. The other three were Abe Kibler, Dr. Reuben Colbert and Ned Hansen, a banker. The emergency meeting took place at the far end of the counter that ran across the side wall of Abe's General Store. Though not a member of the council, Bo Jefferson was in attendance to hold the Bible Thad Jarrett would take the oath on.

Through the brief proceedings, Thad was focused on Abe Kibler. The store owner's head was still heavily bandaged because of the assault he had suffered. Abe's movements were slow and unnatural as if he were moving underwater. Abe stood throughout the meeting but tightly gripped the counter. Balance had obviously become a problem for the man.

Immediately after Thad removed his hand from the Bible, his half-brother spoke to him. "Normally, I would pin the badge on you right now. But the circumstances aren't normal. Your first job as sheriff is to inform Quaid Markham he's been relieved of duty. You'll take the badge from him—"

"Jus' a moment, Zeke," Abe protested. "Takin' his badge from a jasper like Markham ain't like puttin' cans on a shelf. No sir. One of the council members needs to go along with Thad and tell that buzzard what's up. Make it official, like." He began to untie the long apron that draped his body. "Won't hurt me none to shut down for a few minutes and—"

Zeke Darcel eyed the other two council members now staring at him. He waved a nervous hand at the store owner. "You're right, Abe. Shoulda' thought of such matters myself. I'll go along with Thad." He paused, then added, "Hell, I'll enjoy telling Quaid Markham he's through."

Darcel's attempt at bravado didn't work. He

pressed his lips together as his eyes beamed fear. Still, he walked out of Abe's General Store with Jarrett and Jefferson and the threesome began a journey along the boardwalk toward the sheriff's office.

Thad mused briefly on the unusual status of the pastor of Travis' only church. Bo Jefferson now had a gun holstered on his hip. Everyone at the hastily called meeting had just assumed the pastor would accompany Thad on his dangerous mission. Before they left the store, Bo had handed his Bible to Kibler. "Could you keep this for me, Abe? I'll be back in a few minutes."

"Honored to, Preacher."

Reflections on that moment shifted Thad's thoughts. He spoke softly to Jefferson. "Abe didn't look very healthy."

"He's not," Bo replied crisply. "Doctor Colbert says he can't do anything about Abe's loss of balance. Abe also has awful dizzy spells. The doctor doesn't think Abe is going to live much longer."

Anger flamed in Thad Jarrett's face. He started walking faster. "That's not right. Not right at all."

Bo nodded in agreement. "This town owes Abe Kibler a lot. The way he extends credit to folks who can't afford food and other necessities. I know some of his so-called customers have never paid him back in full."

The sheriff's office was coming into sight. "I

intend to do some paying back right now," Jarrett declared.

As they got closer to the office, a blocky man with a scraggly brown beard was pausing at the office's door. "That's Deputy Hoke," sarcasm permeated Jefferson's voice.

Hoke studied the approaching threesome, then scrambled inside the office. Jarrett laughed at the sight. "Looks like Hoke is announcing our visit."

Thad glanced at his half-brother. Zeke's hands were trembling. But he kept walking forward. In his own way, Zeke Darcel was displaying courage.

The three men paused at the door to the sheriff's office, exchanged nods, then entered.

Sheriff Quaid Markham sat behind his desk. His body slumped casually in a wooden chair as if nothing important was happening. Stubble covered a face with a pinched mouth and hard eyes. Markham moved his left hand about as he spoke; his right hand remained under the desk, out of sight.

"Well, well, Hoke, this here is our lucky day. We got a member of the town council and the preacher visitin' us and it seems they brought them along a guest. Dunt you feel lucky?"

"Yeh." Hoke now stood a few feet to the right of his boss' desk, a rifle cradled in his arms. He stroked the Henry affectionately as if it were an infant.

Zeke Darcel's voice was higher pitched than usual but still firm. "Sheriff Markham, Deputy Hoke, you are now both relieved of your duties." Zeke held both arms behind his back to stop them from shaking. "Thad Jarrett will take over as sheriff beginning immediately." He paused, then added as an afterthought, "Reverend Jefferson, an outstanding citizen of our town, will no doubt assist the new sheriff until an appropriate candidate for deputy can be found."

Markham's laugh was loud and harsh. "My, my, Zeke, you kin sure come up with proper words. Guess that's about all you're good for."

Jarrett spoke for the first time since entering the office. "Mr. Darcel has done a fine job." He motioned toward the door. "Your duty here is finished, Sir. Bo and I can put out the trash by ourselves."

Gratitude calmed the terror twisting through Zeke Darcel's soul. He mumbled a "thank you" and hurried out of the office.

Thad's eyes never left Quaid Markham, whose right hand remained under his desk. With Zeke gone, there would be no witnesses to claim otherwise if Markham were to assert that he had to kill two intruders.

The new sheriff's voice sounded cold and emotionless. "Markham, you and Hoke are to put your badges and guns on the desk and ride out of Travis immediately."

Markham's body remained slumped in a guise of casualness. "Hoke, I dunt much feel like leavin' town, how 'bout you?"

"Same." Hoke's grip on the Henry tightened.

Markham shifted slightly in his chair. Jarrett bolted forward, grabbed the desk, and pushed it into Markham as he fired the pistol in his right hand. The bullet burrowed into the floor. Markham's gun dropped on top of it, neatly covering the bullet hole.

Jefferson drew his gun and shouted at the deputy. "Throw down the rifle, now!"

The rifle clattered against the floor as Jarrett grabbed Markham by his shirt collar, slammed him into the wall behind his desk and pounded his head with a series of vicious blows. He then stood back and glared at the crooked lawman, who was now splayed against the wall.

"You're real good at assaulting an old man from behind, Quaid." Both of Thad's hands were clenched into fists. "Let's see you pick on someone your own age."

Quaid Markham's breathing was ragged. He said nothing.

Thad quickly took in the situation around him. Bo Jefferson had relieved Hoke of his gun, leaving an empty holster. "I'm giving you a onetime offer, Hoke," the pastor snapped. "Ride out of town and never come back. Otherwise, you're destined for a jail cell."

"Whadda ya chargin' me with?"

"I'm sure a few conversations with the citizens of Travis who you have beaten and threatened will provide enough information to keep you behind bars for years." The anger in Bo's voice rose. "Last chance."

Hoke tossed his badge onto the desk and scrambled out the office door. Cheers accompanied the hoofbeats as Hoke galloped out of town. A crowd had gathered on the boardwalk across the street.

The presence of the spectators elevated Thad's spirits. Now he could give Quaid Markham at least part of what he deserved.

Being careful not to allow the crooked lawman to fall, Jarrett grabbed him by his collar and walked him out of the office into the middle of the dusty street. Markham wavered a bit as Thad let go of him and then pulled the badge off his gun belt which now held an empty holster. While smirking at Quaid Markham, the new sheriff pinned the badge onto his own shirt. He then took several steps back.

Jarrett unbuckled his gun belt and let it drop to the ground. "We're both unarmed, Quaid, so let's settle our differences with fists."

Markham moved his lips, but no words came out.

Thad advanced toward his prey. "Speak up, Quaid! I can't hear you!"

Fearful and humiliated, Markham let out a screech of profanity. Thad responded with a brutal assault to the crooked lawman's face. Blood wormed from Markham's nose onto the dust as he now lay collapsed in the street.

"Get up, Markham!" Jarrett took a few steps back, preparing for a kick to his victim's ribs. "I said, get up!"

A strong hand suddenly grabbed Jarrett's shoulder. "That's enough, Thad." Bo Jefferson looked at the crowd on the boardwalk and gestured to Doc Colbert.

The doctor hurried to the fallen thug and crouched over him. The physician seemed overwhelmed by the irony of the situation. A man who had only an hour ago held the town in terror was now no threat at all. Amusement laced his voice. "Our former sheriff will need some patching, but he should be able to saddle up and leave town in a few hours."

"Obliged if you let me know when, Doc," Jarrett said.

Colbert was still enjoying the moment. "My pleasure."

Jefferson shouted at the crowd. "Doctor Colbert will need help getting this man to his office."

Several men almost jumped off the boardwalk and hurried to volunteer. They now wanted to be part of an important and happy event in the life of Travis, Arizona.

Thad Jarrett and Bo Jefferson remained standing together in the middle of the street as they watched Quaid Markham being carried off.

"I'm gonna need your help, Preacher."

"Sure. Like Zeke said, I can serve as your deputy until you find someone to handle it full time."

"Obliged," Jarrett responded softly. "But I'm needing more than that."

"I don't follow you."

"You saw how I jus' acted," Jarrett explained. "Two years of being a hired gun has unleashed a demon inside me. A lawman needs a cool head. Think you can help me get that demon back in his cage?"

Bo Jefferson nodded his head. "You've come to the right man. Turns out, I've wrestled with some demons myself."

CHAPTER FIVE

Twenty-Two Years Later

Kain Arnell checked the time in the train station. It was five minutes until eight in the morning. His boss valued punctuality. Kain hastily left the station and headed for the almost empty train sitting majestically on the tracks several yards away. The train would be there until Bradford Conrad, the president of Conrad Western Railroad, ordered it to leave.

Kain entered the train, finding the first passenger car empty save for two guards who nodded at him as if happy to have something to do. The second car contained no human residents but still sparkled. This was the dining car where Bradford Conrad entertained guests. Kain marveled at how the tablecloths remained a bright white.

The cook responsible for the miracle was in the next car, a kitchen. Kain had forgotten the cook's name, but the man smiled nervously at him as he passed through.

Kain Arnell was a boyishly handsome man in his early twenties. Clean shaven with sandy hair, he appeared to be a model of wholesomeness. Any mother would be pleased if her daughter were to attend the Saturday night barn dance with him.

Mom wouldn't be so happy to learn Kain Arnell was a killer for hire. He wasn't the kind who got his name in the newspapers. No gunfights in the middle of the street for Kain. He killed his victims from a distance, or pressed a gun in their back, fired and left town while the law was still trying to find out where the shot had come from.

Kain entered the office area of the train. There were usually two or three workers present. Today, there was only one: Draper Collins, Conrad's confidential secretary.

"Good morning, Mr. Arnell," Collins addressed him respectfully. "Mr. Conrad is expecting you, go right in."

The next car was the first one on the train that reflected any personality. Not that the personality was particularly good. Cigarette smoke drifted about looking for a place to settle. A rumpled sofa that doubled as a bed ran across one side of the space. On the other side were three chairs and some tables, cluttered with newspapers, magazines, and dime novels.

In the center, a huge desk dominated the car. The desktop was a maze of papers, with a large ashtray and an ornate ink pen holder protruding above the papers as if gasping for air.

Bradford Conrad sat behind the desk. He was a man in his early fifties, with deep set eyes. The rest of his face appeared haggard, like a man who had been fasting. Conrad was a man of average height with brown and gray hair in a condition of permanent retreat.

"Sit down," Conrad greeted. The hired killer obeyed, tossing a stack of newspapers off a chair near the desk and settling in.

"Is he dead?" the boss asked.

"Yes."

"Funny thing," Conrad remarked, his voice not betraying a trace of amusement. "If the law knew what you done, they'd hang you. Hell! How many chinks do you suppose I worked to death? How many others got sick or injured and left by the wayside to die? The law doesn't give a hoot 'bout none of that."

Conrad inhaled on a cigarette and slowly exhaled. To Kain the smoke seemed to come from the man's soul.

"All the good citizens care 'bout is getting the railroad built," Conrad continued. "They don't wanna be bothered with details."

The tycoon crushed his cigarette into the ashtray. Ashes and a few cigarette butts flowed over onto his desk. Conrad picked up the tray and emptied it into a wastebasket beside the desk.

"Got a full staff coming in later," Conrad explained while returning the ashtray to its place. "We're pulling out for Phoenix first thing tomorra' morning. Got an appointment with a senator; will have to get the cleaning folks to do this car. Hate that."

Bradford Conrad looked confused, as if trying to decipher why cleaning up his private office bothered him. Deciding to forget the matter, he pulled a package of Sportsman's Caporals from his shirt pocket and fired up another smoke.

Kain reckoned his boss was one of the very few men in the Territory who smoked premade cigarettes. He mused to himself that it might be a necessity. Bradford Conrad chain smoked. Hand rolling his own cigarettes would consume half a day.

"Your next job will be in Travis."

"Who do I kill?"

"Nobody. Next month the good folk of Travis are voting on a referendum, know what that is?"

Kain Arnell was surprised by the question but not bothered by it. "Sure. A referendum is when people vote to do or not do something."

The killer's boss smiled approvingly. "You got it. In the case of Travis, they are voting on whether to try and get the railroad to come through their fair town."

The gunman looked confused. "Where do I fit in?"

Conrad flicked a spray of red embers in the direction of the ashtray. "I like you, Arnell. You're vicious and deadly, but no one would know it. You look good. You talk good. Go to Travis and be a politician: shake hands, pass out candy to the kids, make speeches. Tell all those cow lovers how a railroad will make them rich."

"And I don't have to kill anyone?"

This time, Conrad's amusement was genuine. "Maybe not. I'll leave the details to you."

Anxiety tinged the gunman's voice. "Thad Jarrett is sheriff of Travis."

"You know 'bout Jarrett . . ."

Kain waved a hand at the books scattered around the car. "I read dime novels, too."

"Yep. Thad Jarrett bringing down Music Matt McCall is still the stuff of stories and songs. So is a lot of other stuff he's done."

"From what I hear, Jarrett is still one of the toughest lawdogs in the Territory."

"Right on top of the heap with Wyatt Earp," Conrad agreed. "But Jarrett may not have an eye for the kind of lawbreaking you'll carry out in Travis. Don't jus' pass out candy to kids. There may be a few grown up jaspers with itchy palms who can help with that election." Conrad barked a laugh. "Like ever'thing else valuable, votes can be bought."

Kain fidgeted with his hands. "Think we'll have serious trouble from the opposition?"

Bradford Conrad nodded his head. "Yep. There're always folks who want things to stay the same. Then there's the Pacific National Line."

"Pacific wants to run through Travis?"

"No. They don't need it. But they want to stop

us. Hell, they want to destroy us. We're their main competition."

Conrad picked up a newspaper from his desk and tossed it to his henchman. "But the buzzards at Pacific haven't clued in that times are changing. Look at the paper."

Kain picked up the copy of the *Dallas Herald*. One quarter of the front page consisted of a cartoon showing three comically bloated men. Across each man's stomach appeared the name of a railroad. The caricatures were holding the strings of three marionettes. From left to right the marionettes were marked: Washington, The States, and The Territories.

Kain gave his boss a confused look.

Conrad responded with a contented smile. "Notice that Pacific National is one of those fat guys, but not Conrad Western Railroad."

The henchman still didn't understand. "Yeh, that's good . . ."

"We've been tougher than all of them, but we still kept our noses clean, know how?"

Kain had never seen the boss man so joyful. He smiled weakly and shrugged his shoulders.

"I know when to fight and when not to fight," Conrad bragged. "This railroad never cheated anyone out of land. We always pay market value. And that saves us money, know how?"

Conrad knew his hired killer didn't have the answer, so he provided it. "Take a man's land from him and he gets downright ornery. He sets fires, blows things up, does all kinds of sabotage that delays building."

The tycoon inhaled his cigarette, then blew out a stream of smoke. The process seemed to lift his spirits even higher. "Now, it's paying off. We're one of the angels." He waved a hand in the direction of the office Kain had just walked through. "Hell, you should read the stuff Draper Collins feeds to the newspapers. Conrad Western Railroad is the Railroad with a heart. We care about the brave and noble settlers who are taming the West. We want to be their servant!"

Bradford Conrad paused and looked at the ceiling as if studying the heavens. "The reporters don't know it yet, but the governor of the Territory is sick. Really sick. He'll be stepping down soon."

Kain Arnell's eyes widened. Suddenly, all the boss' talk made sense. "You're going to be appointed Governor of the Arizona Territory!?"

"Maybe." Conrad's voice became a warning. "We've got to play our cards smart. Very smart. Our railroad needs to run through Travis. Make sure it happens. But be an angel when you do."

"What if I have to be an angel of death?"

The contented smile returned to Bradford Conrad's face. "Be as nice about it as you can."

CHAPTER SIX

Travis, Arizona's two schoolteachers stood on the porch of the schoolhouse on each side of a sign they had painted the previous night. The white sign stood over six feet high with red lettering which pleaded: "Vote No on Railroad Referendum."

Link and Tracey Bonner had come to Travis three years back to take charge of educating the town's children. Link Bonner was the opposite of the skinny Ichabod Crane picture of a teacher. Well above average height, Link had a hefty build which was still short of being overweight. His stentorian voice and carefully trimmed black beard lent him an authoritarian air, though he could be lighthearted and cheerful with his students when they were being well behaved.

Tracey was more in range of the schoolmarm image. Standing at a little over five feet, she had blondish brown hair which framed a pretty but frail appearing face. Even in the August of a hot Arizona summer, Tracey's countenance was a pale white. But Tracey always came across as energetic. The woman impressed many as employing enthusiasm to compensate for poor health. At twenty-eight she was two years younger than her husband.

Tracey and Link looked across the sign at each other. Over thirty people were gathered in front of the schoolhouse, which was located on the northern edge of Travis. It was time to get started.

"Good Afternoon!" Link shouted. Several people shouted the same back at him. Link gave the assembled a friendly wave, then continued. "Most of you know that Tracey and I are heading up the opposition to bringing a railroad into Travis. Of course, we are aware of the advantages such a move would have for some in our community. Still, we must carefully—"

A bullet pierced the sign, causing it to wobble. A second shot sent the wooden object slamming onto the porch.

People began to shout and scream. Horses tied up at the hitch rail in front of the school whinnied with fear and pulled at their reins.

Link held up his arms, trying to calm the crowd. He yelled angrily at the man who sat on a large gray directly behind the crowd. "What is the meaning of this, Varn Tobin?!"

Tobin smiled in a cocky manner and blew on the wisps of smoke coming out of his Remington Army .44. "Hell, Schoolteacher, I'm jus' practicin' my rights. In a dee-mocracy, a man's gotta right to disagree."

Tracey's voice was defiant. "You care nothing about democracy, Tobin, and you care nothing about this town or the people in it. Who's paying you to stop this rally?"

Thick black stubble covered Tobin's face and black hair ran well past his collar. A lewd expression replaced the cockiness in his eyes. "You got a problem, don't you lady? From what I hear tell, you can't have pups of your own, so you console yourself with bein' a schoolmarm. What ya need ta do is jus' relax. Yep, jus' take it easy, enjoy yourself and before ya know it, you'll have a litter."

"You rotten buzzard!" Link jumped off the porch and ran with remarkable speed at the gunman. Tobin fired a third shot. Link hit the ground. The panicked crowd scattered.

Stacey Hooper patted the neck of his horse. "I think my trusty steed is almost as thirsty as I am, Rance. Of course, we thirst for much different beverages."

"Travis is only about fifteen minutes away," Rance Dehner assured.

The bright sun above brought Hooper no joy. "As I understand it, you are spending your vacation in a town Beelzebub would consider a tad too warm, in order to perform an act of charity for a friend."

"Wrong," Dehner quickly replied. "I'm repaying a debt. Six months ago, Sheriff Thad Jarrett helped me uncover the Grange brothers, three dangerous killers hiding out in the area of Travis. We brought two of them in alive, one across his saddle. Thad put his own life on the line. I owe him."

Hooper smiled approvingly. "I must confess, I am looking forward to meeting the Sheriff of Travis. The man is a legend in his own time."

Dehner nodded agreement. "Those dime novel writers and newspaper reporters actually got it right with Thad Jarrett."

"From what I've read, Jarrett became a lawman in Travis just as the war between the states was breaking out."

"Yes. Arizona, of course, stayed out of the war. But there was plenty of intrigue going on in this territory carried out by both sides. Thad protected his town from all that. After the war, he dealt with the large number of settlers moving west."

"He's been a most busy man."

"He still is," Dehner added. "But Thad found time to help a detective from the Lowrie Agency and made him look good to his boss."

The town was starting to come into view. Hooper continued to shuffle matters about in his mind. "But now, our famed lawman needs help with a vote that's coming up?"

Both men could now spot a building which looked like a schoolhouse. A group of people was huddled in front of it. "One week from tomorrow, the citizens of Travis are voting on a referendum," Dehner explained. "They will decide on whether the town should be open to having a railroad come through."

They were now close enough to Travis to confirm that the building was a school. Dehner wondered if the meeting going on was a political rally of some kind.

Hooper shrugged his shoulders. "I can't understand the controversy. A railroad always brings riches to a location, along with a variety of delightful advantages."

Dehner tilted his head sideways in a thoughtful manner. "A railroad changes a town completely. Suddenly there is a surge of gambling, drunkenness, violence, and prostitution. Hordes of card sharks, grifters and dreamers invade."

"Indeed! As I just said, 'a variety of delightful advantages.' Though, from what I hear, Travis is already a prosperous cow town. I must confess, my reasons for accompanying you, Rance, are not entirely altruistic. I don't care how a man votes. If he's got money in his pockets to lose at cards—"

Two shots exploded from the schoolhouse. Dehner spurred his bay into a fast gallop. Hooper kept pace with him.

As the two men came into close sight of the commotion, they spotted one gunman on a horse behind the crowd. The gunney fired a third shot. Neither Dehner nor his companion could tell if anyone had been hit.

Dehner pulled up and palmed his Colt .45. "Throw down your gun, mister. Right now!"

Varn Tobin's shout sounded like a boy on a playground. "Who the hell do ya think ya are, buttin' in? This ain't none of your business!"

Hooper's reply was fast but cordial. "We must leave introductions and matters of propriety until later. I strongly suggest you follow my friend's orders."

"Damn both of ya!" Tobin began to aim his gun at the intruders. Dehner flamed a spear into the gunman's shoulder.

Tobin screamed in pain, dropping his .44. For a moment Tobin stared at the gun in wonderment as if pondering the irony of a weapon so close being unattainable. The gunney quickly awoke to the moment, turned his gray, and began a fast ride into town.

Dehner pointed at the mass of confusion in front of the school. "See if you can help these folks, Stacey." Dehner galloped after the thug.

Riding into Travis, Tobin gave a loud whoop as he spotted a stagecoach leaving the station. He almost trampled over a man crossing the street as he pulled even with the coach. Ignoring the curses being hurled at him from his near victim, Tobin drew even with the stage and spurred his gray viciously.

Pulling in front of the stagecoach, Tobin was certain he was out of sight of his pursuer. At first opportunity, he yanked his steed into a right turn and created a dust cloud as he hurtled down another, less crowded street. This street ran forever, becoming a large path outside of Travis. Varn Tobin could taste escape.

Adrenaline can only work for so long. The burn in Tobin's shoulder became increasingly wide and painful. There was nothing he could do to stem the flow of blood running down his right side. The world began to spin as he plunged from his horse.

Varn Tobin hit the ground and began to bounce as a boot remained stuck in a stirrup. His head collided with patches of small stones. Consciousness had begun to slip away when suddenly the gray stopped.

Rance Dehner dismounted and freed Tobin's booted foot. A man in bib overalls approached the detective. "Say fella, wasn't ya here before?"

"Yes." Dehner crouched down and examined the gunney.

"As I recall, you was after some owlhoots."

"Yes."

The questioner laughed. "Guess you jus' always git into trouble."

"Guess so," Dehner replied. "Could you help me get this man to a doctor?"

CHAPTER SEVEN

Sheriff Thad Jarrett, Rance Dehner and Stacey Hooper toted the prisoner into a jail cell. With a nominal display of gentleness, they had Varn Tobin lying down more or less comfortably on the jail cell's cot.

As he had since they carried him in a buckwagon from the doctor's house, Tobin mumbled curses at his three captors. But the curses were delivered in a faint whisper.

"The doc says you'll be fine in the morning," Jarrett declared in a mock friendly manner. "We'll have ourselves a great conversation over breakfast."

By the time Jarrett was locking the cell door, the prisoner was asleep. "Thanks gents," the lawman smiled broadly at his two companions. "We've all been a bit busy since I discovered Rance toting this buzzard over to the doc's. Guess I never did give you a formal welcome to Travis."

"I suspect the welcome we received at the town's schoolhouse was indicative of what is to come during our stay," Stacey's smile was even broader.

"Guess so," Thad agreed, "let's talk with the Bonners, then I'll swear you gents in as volunteer deputies."

Thad Jarrett had a muscular build with a face still handsome despite the lines accrued from many years spent in the hot sun. He led his soon-to-be deputies out of the jail area and into the office where Deputy Farley Canton was standing behind the office's one desk, talking earnestly with the town's two schoolteachers.

Farley was twenty-one with tawny hair and a lantern jaw. When speaking to the sheriff, he always sounded anxious to please. Having a living legend as your boss could be tough.

"I jus' tole the Bonners they need to fill out a complaint on Varn Tobin, then—"

"They got ever' right to make a complaint," Thad interrupted. "But I hope they don't."

Farley looked embarrassed. The Bonners looked shocked.

Sheriff Jarrett answered the couple's unspoken question. "Varn Tobin is a stupid thug who doesn't give a hoot 'bout the railroad. When you charged at him, Link, he fired near your feet. Someone paid Tobin to hooraw your meeting but not to hurt anyone."

"Yes, Sheriff," Tracey snapped, "and a thug needs to be in prison!"

"He may be more valuable as a free man."

Tracey wasn't satisfied. "Please explain yourself, Sheriff!"

"Varn Tobin ain't much more than an insect and he's got the brain of an insect." Thad waved his hand in the direction of Rance and Stacey. "For a while, I'm gonna have two extra deputies. I think we can keep watch on Tobin and learn who paid him. I'd like to turn him loose in the morning."

Link spoke to his wife. "Makes sense."

Tracey Bonner pressed her lips together and reluctantly nodded her head.

After the couple left the office, Jarrett put a hand on his deputy's shoulder. "Farley, you'll have to uphold law and order by yourself this evening. I'm taking Dehner and Hooper out to the ranch. Treat 'em to a home cooked meal."

"Sure thing, Sheriff."

Thad swore in his temporary deputies and gave them both small pieces of tin. "You gents are gonna get some good eats tonight. But there's also some people you need to meet. Let's get started on that right now."

Reverend Bo Jefferson laughed good-naturedly as he explained to Dehner and Hooper, "I got my name in a few newspapers after the Music Matt McCall incident, but the dime novel writers ignored me. Good thing. One living legend is enough for a town the size of Travis."

As the pastor spoke, Dehner noted the similarities and differences in the two men who were riding with the new deputies. Bo and Thad were both in their mid-forties. Both had once sported dark hair. Bo's hair was now salt and pepper, but in Thad's case the salt was, for the moment, content to remain in his sideburns.

Thad was a lanky man, well over six feet. Bo was average height with a craggy face. Somehow, the pastor carried the aura of a scholar.

After leaving the Sheriff's office, Thad, Rance and Stacey had mounted their horses and ridden to the church, which was on the south side of Travis, forming the second half of a bookend with the school. There they had met Bo Jefferson and the four men began the twenty-minute ride to Jarrett's ranch, the Circle J.

"The upcoming referendum is obviously engendering strong emotions," Stacey's voice indicated amusement at stating the obvious. He glanced at Thad and then Bo. "Are either one of you gentlemen taking a stand on the railroad issue?"

Bo's reply was immediate. "No. Thad and I agree that the town's sheriff and its pastor must stay neutral. We've been entrusted with keeping watch on things at the poll on voting day and then monitoring the vote count. People must trust us to be fair."

Stacey nodded his head. "I can understand the emotional upheaval. Some citizens believe a railroad will bring great riches and streets paved with gold. Others see a descent into sin and decadence. Such entrenched viewpoints allow for little in the way of compromise."

Stacey's remark sparked a wistful look on

the sheriff's face. "Change comes, like it or not." Thad seemed to be speaking primarily to himself. "Travis didn't used to be much more than a settlement. Not anymore. Time scuttles along. The town must now decide what direction it wants to head out for. The decision's gotta be made by the town folks themselves. Not by a handful of jaspers shaking hands and passing out cigars behind closed doors."

Rance silently mused on the sheriff's words. Thad seemed to speak about the town of Travis as if it were a child making the rough transition into adulthood. After twenty years of bringing law to Travis, Rance could understand how Thad Jarrett would feel parental toward the town.

As they rode onto the Circle J, Dehner was amused by Stacey Hooper's wide eyes. The Circle J was a huge spread. Even the bunkhouse and cook's shack were large and impressive.

The ranch house was long and sprawling. A careful look revealed an addition had been recently added. The Circle J screamed success.

As the four men were tying up their horses to a hitch rail in front of the house, Thad pointed to a rider coming in from the ranch's east side. "That's my Cassie!" Jarrett proudly proclaimed.

As Cassie rode past a corral, one of the ranch hands working there abandoned his tasks and walked briskly toward the house. Cassie didn't need to signal him. The ranch hand knew what was expected.

As the young woman pulled up and dismounted, Rance admired the lady's horse. Cassie rode a magnificent black with perfectly matched white stockings. When he had first seen the animal six months back, Dehner had wanted to ask the lady where she got the horse and how much it cost, but good manners forbade.

Cassie Jarrett was even more striking than her steed. Standing at about five and a half feet, the lady boasted a figure that no doubt turned heads. Reddish brown hair surrounded a lovely face with an almost perfect complexion. Her blue eyes added to the charm.

But those eyes did not gleam with playfulness. A serious quality radiated from the beautiful face of the twenty-year old Cassie Jarrett.

"Rance, it is good to see you again." The woman first shook hands with Dehner and then with Stacey Hooper. She was polite and mechanical. Introductions were common in Cassie Jarrett's life.

Bo Jefferson's voice was a tease. "Young lady, you've collected even more dust today than usual. Are the cows being more ornery than usual?"

"Men are more trouble than cows," the woman sounded as if she were only half-joking. "We're having to build two new line shacks along the eastern border of the ranch, near the land where the homesteaders farm. I had to help. I guess sitting in a saddle and serenading cattle has made some waddies worthless when it comes to a hammer and nails."

Cassie's horse nickered. The woman turned and gave a casual "Thanks, Trey," to the ranch hand who had walked from the corral and was now taking her black to the stable. She then returned her gaze to Thad. "Father, why don't you fix our guests some drinks? I'll brush off and check with the cook. Dinner should be ready in about a half-hour."

Dinner was indeed ready in almost exactly thirty minutes. It was a delicious meal served in a fine dining room. Dehner noted that Cassie Jarrett communicated with the kitchen staff by using hand signals and occasionally moving her lips with silent instructions.

Thad sat at the head of the table with Bo on his immediate right and Cassie sitting beside the pastor. Rance and Stacey were seated to the left of the sheriff.

The group was enjoying a dessert of peach pie when Stacey shook his head in amazement. "Thad, the dime novelists do not do you justice. Not only are you an outstanding lawman, but you also run a magnificent ranch."

Thad surprised his guests by blushing. "I have nothing to do with the success of the Circle J." He took a sip of coffee, then continued. "After

Cassie was born, my wife Linda and I decided to start a small ten head ranch to bring in some extra money. Linda surprised both of us by being quite a business lady. While I was in town locking up barflies, Linda was creating a huge, prosperous ranch."

Thad used his fork to cut off a piece of pie, which he then left on the plate. "When Linda died two years ago, I was going to sell the ranch. But Cassie stepped up and took charge. My daughter inherited her mother's smarts and her ability to handle hard work. So, it's the women in the family who have made us rich. I sure had nothing to do with it."

Cassie cut in immediately. "That's not true, Father! If it hadn't been for you, the Circle J would have become a pile of rubble and spilled blood." She turned to the man sitting beside her. "Bo, you went through all that with Father. Please tell our guests the full story."

Bo Jefferson sighed deeply. "The story of the Arizona Territory is a story about struggles over land. First came the cattle barons battling over grazing land. After the war between the states, the situation really turned dangerous. Homesteaders moved in. The law was on their side, but the cattlemen hated them. Imagine, using valuable land for farming! The cattlemen's first instinct was to drive them out by any means necessary."

Cassie cut in proudly. "But Thad Jarrett had different ideas."

Bo smiled in agreement and continued. "Thad called a meeting of the Cattlemen's Association and invited the homesteaders to attend. He delivered a more powerful sermon than I ever preached. He told the ranch owners that if they threatened the farmers, he would jail them. But he also told the homesteaders they needed to respect the cattlemen. The ranchers were here first."

The pastor laughed lightly. "I always try to have a practical side to my preaching. Thad beat me in that regard. Our sheriff presented a plan for dividing up land between the homesteaders and the cattlemen. Including a way to handle newcomers."

"Did everyone agree to it?" Dehner asked.

"Almost everyone," Jefferson answered. "Moss Storey planned to show Thad who was boss. Moss owned a huge spread at the time and ordered a homesteader to leave or be burned out. Fortunately, one of Moss' ranch hands had a crush on the homesteader's daughter. He went to the law. Thad and a group of concerned citizens were waiting for Moss and his boys the next night."

"You were one of those concerned citizens, Bo," Thad added.

The pastor waved a hand as if brushing off

an insignificant fact. "The trial of Moss Storey and his thugs created quite a stir in these parts. They all got long jail sentences. The authority of the sheriff of Travis in matters of land was established."

Cassie smiled at her father, then looked at her two guests. "I was too young at the time to understand what was going on. But Mother told me all about it. Father established peace and stability in this area. He made it possible for ranchers to be successful and for homesteaders to . . . homestead."

Thad Jarrett's face once again went red. "Rance and Stacey, you'll have to forgive my daughter and friend. They don't usually apple polish."

"Enough, Father!" Cassie ordered playfully. "And all that nonsense you mentioned about not making much money. Why, you could have a job that pays more than triple what you earn now."

"I'm where I belong." Thad's reply was quick. He obviously wanted to close the matter.

Cassie wouldn't let it close. The playfulness vanished from her voice. "But Father, that position in St. Louis pays well and it's a desk job. You've already faced more danger in your life than ten men. How much longer can your luck hold out?! And you're not getting any younger—"

"I'm where I belong."

The young woman sighed deeply. She lifted a napkin from her lap, placed it on the table, and spoke in a stiff, formal manner. "You gentlemen will have to excuse me. I need to change clothes. I have a meeting in town tonight with Reade Bourke and a representative of the Conrad Western Railroad, Kain Arnell. Father may think it wrong to take a stand for progress and modern ways. I do not. I wish you all a pleasant evening."

Cassie Jarrett didn't stomp out of the room, but she came close to it.

"Sorry," Thad whispered. "That was my fault."

Bo tried to sound comforting. "It's nobody's fault, Thad. This railroad business has everyone on edge. Your family isn't the only one being divided. One way or another it will all be over soon."

"The voting will be done soon," the sheriff confirmed. "But as for all the bitterness and conflict, I'm not sure about that. Not sure at all."

Dehner thought it might help to ask a factual question. "Who is Reade Bourke?"

A wistful expression covered Thad's face. "Zeke Darcel left for the East more than a decade back. He sold the ranch to a family from Kansas, the Bourkes. They changed the name of the ranch to the Lazy B. Amos Bourke ran the place until a few years ago, then his son Reade took over. A nice enough boy. I should have said, 'young man.' Reade is the mayor of Travis. He and Cassie have been meeting with this Kain jasper for a few weeks now."

"Kain has attended church regularly since arriving in town," Bo informed. "A very friendly man."

"Yeh, real friendly," the lawman reluctantly agreed. "Look, why don't you gents light a shuck. I'll ride into town with my daughter. Maybe I can get us back to where she'll smile at me now and again."

Bo, Stacey and Rance tossed off forced, cheerful remarks as they departed. Outside the dining room, Dehner glanced back at the sheriff. Thad Jarrett looked tense. He loved his daughter, but she had left him feeling lost and alone.

CHAPTER EIGHT

Bo Jefferson led his chestnut into the small stable behind his house. As he tended to the animal, he whispered a prayer for Thad, Cassie, and the town. He feared his friend was right. The referendum over the railroad had ignited hatred and division which wasn't likely to end with the vote.

"See you in the morning." The pastor gave the chestnut an affectionate pat and then made the short walk to his house, which wasn't much bigger than the stable built for two horses maximum.

The small house was located next to the Travis Community Church. For a long spell, Bo had lived in the church, sleeping in the church office. After he had saved up enough money to put up a house, members of the congregation had helped him build it.

Inside the house, he lit the lantern, which was suspended from a nail beside the door. He carried the lantern to a nearby table. Before he could set it down, he had to push aside a pile of papers consisting of pencil drawings of various Biblical stories.

His house was used for a Sunday School class on Sunday mornings. Bo remembered when the head of the Sunday School, Ida Akers, had asked, no, commanded him regarding the use of his house. "Your living room is perfect for instructing our children. And never forget, Preacher, we *did* help you build the place."

Bo took his coat off and placed it on one of several chairs which were used by the kids. He unbuttoned his vest, untied his cravat, and placed it on top of the coat.

The pastor walked across the room to the sofa which lined one side wall. He flopped down and instinctively reached toward the kerosene lamp and the object beside it. He always read the good book before turning in. But fatigue checked the nightly ritual. He withdrew his hand.

The day had been long and the evening meal at the Circle J had been an emotional wrench. After getting back to town, Bo had left his two companions and ridden around alone. Being by himself on horseback helped the pastor with his prayer life.

Eyes closed, the pastor's thoughts weaved away from the present and dipped deeply into the past. Samantha Preston had looked very much like Cassie Jarrett, only she was even more beautiful.

"At least, that's how I remember her," Bo mumbled wearily. Samantha was the only woman he had ever loved. She had turned him down in favor of a banker, Ned Hansen. The last he had heard, they were living in Houston. "Samantha

73

probably has a passel of kids by now," Bo's second mumble was almost incoherent. "She might . . . be . . . grandmother . . ."

Footsteps from outside awakened the pastor. A flickering light collapsing into what little kerosene was left in the lantern alerted Bo. He had been asleep for several hours. What he heard next chilled him to the core.

"When the trumpet of the Lord shall sound and time shall be no more, and the morning breaks eternal bright and fair . . ."

Bo Jefferson silently cursed his fear. Of course that voice couldn't be coming from Matt McCall. Everyone knew about McCall's vow to return and seek vengeance. Whoever was outside was playing some crazy prank.

"When the saved of earth shall gather over on the other shore . . ."

The voice seemed to be coming from behind the house. Using the front door, the only door, Bo stepped outside. There was no porch. Gravel provided the only threat of giving him away.

". . . and the roll is called up yonder I'll be there."

Bo Jefferson moved quietly around to the side of the house and crept towards the back. He needed to be cautious. The night sky provided no moon or stars. A kicked rock could give him away. As he neared his destination he broke into a run, hoping to surprise whoever it was. His hope was shattered. Jefferson saw the outline of a man singing at the corner of the house opposite him.

"When his chosen ones shall gather to their home beyond the skies . . ." The figure stopped singing. "Well, hello Brother. I have once again come to bring justice. I hope you will step aside and not stand in my way."

"What's going on—"

Jefferson's head seemed to explode. He dropped to the ground, fighting for consciousness. Small, sharp stones cut his forehead. Cold iron pressed against the back of his neck.

A harsh, raspy voice spoke from over him. "I'll tell you what's goin' on, Preacher Man. Music Matt McCall is back."

Even lying face down with blood seeping out of his head, Bo Jefferson couldn't let that pass. "Only one man has ever conquered death, and it isn't Matt McCall."

The raspy voice continued. "You talk a lot 'bout good news, Sky Pilot. Well, here's some news you may not find so good. Matt McCall had a son. Yep. Matt McCall's boy is livin' right here in Travis under another name. He thinks it's time to get revenge for the old man."

"Starting with me."

"No Sky Pilot, Matt's son is gonna let you live . . . for a while. He wants you to be a messenger."

"And just what's the message?"

"Tell Thad Jarrett to leave town. Forever. He can take one of them fancy jobs he's been offered. He needs to be gone tomorrow before noon, or else."

"Or else what?"

"Matt's son knows Jarrett real good. Knows how to hurt him. If Jarrett stays in town people die. First dead body may not be so hard to take. But each killing will get closer and closer to the good sheriff. McCall's got plenty of friends to back up his threats. Can you tell Jarrett that?"

"Yes, but—"

"Here's more proof of our sincerity!"

A second explosion flashed red across Bo's eyes, then there was darkness.

"Git up, Reverent! Ya cain't sleep on the ground. The law will come along and kick your feet. I know!"

Bo Jefferson was lying face down. He slowly and cautiously rolled over. In the gray of early morning, he saw a familiar figure standing over him. "Ah . . . hello . . . Billy."

Billy was a man of indeterminate age. He was portly with a ruddy face. He always wore shoddy clothes. His head was topped by a derby with part of the brim missing.

"Let me help ya up."

Bo grabbed the hand that was offered to him

and was pulled onto his feet. Billy's arm was surprisingly strong. For the first time it occurred to the pastor that of all the freeloaders in town, Billy was the only one who qualified as fat.

The insight was brushed away by a sudden onslaught of nausea. Bo jackknifed, holding on to consciousness.

"Seems like ya had you'self a ree-el bad night, Reverent."

"A crazy man attacked me. Claimed Matt McCall's son was in Travis. Planned killings if Sheriff Jarrett didn't leave town."

Bo spotted drops of blood falling onto the ground. "I have to get to the doctor."

He straightened up and began to fall backwards. Billy caught him.

"You're is gonna need plenty help to git to Doc Raikin's place. He's way on the other side of town near the school. Be happy to help ya, Reverent."

"Obliged," Jefferson spoke as he pulled a handkerchief from his pocket and pressed it against one of the wounds on his head.

"Let's git ya to your stable. We can ride double to the doc's."

"Obliged." Jefferson repeated.

They began a slow trek to the stable, Billy holding on to the pastor's arm. "Ya know, Reverent, it's lucky for ya that I am up and about this mornin'."

"Yes."

"A lotta folks is still in bed or jus' gittin' up. They ain't much help to ya."

"I'm grateful, Billy." Jefferson's steps were becoming a little more certain.

"Don't it say somewhere in the good book that a man should git paid for doin' work?"

Bo Jefferson caught the drift. "How about twenty-five cents?"

"Well now, that'll buy a man a beer. 'Course, a man likes ta be sociable when he's drinkin'. Cain't be very sociable with jus' one beer."

"Fifty cents."

"That's good of ya, Reverent."

Billy opened the stable door and helped Jefferson inside. The pastor leaned against a wall while Billy saddled his horse.

Bo removed his bloodied handkerchief from his head. He folded it and began to return it to the wound when he spotted an object tied around his wrist. The pastor's body stiffened in terror.

CHAPTER NINE

Bo Jefferson stood in the sheriff's office explaining the events of the previous night. He had an audience of four: Thad Jarrett, Deputy Farley Canton, and volunteer deputies Rance Dehner and Stacey Hooper.

After recounting most of his story, Jefferson glanced out the window at the dimming sunlight. "Horace Raikin ordered me to lay down in his surgery for a spell. I just woke up an hour ago." The pastor touched his bandaged head lightly. "I slept right through that noon deadline I was supposed to give you, Thad."

The sheriff responded slowly. He was processing what he had just been told. "Those jaspers knew I wouldn't saddle up and make dust out of Travis. That was just a first move on the checkerboard. They're planning to get rid of me—somehow."

Jarrett appeared to look at nothing at all, then he looked at his old friend. "How many men do you suppose attacked you?"

"I think there were three in all, judging by the footsteps I heard. I tried to get the . . . well . . . I'll say 'lost soul,' who hit me, to talk a lot. But I didn't recognize his voice. And I didn't recognize the singing voice. The jasper sang off-key, but so does three quarters of my congregation."

The pastor smirked at his last remark and then continued. "There is one more thing. When I regained consciousness, this was on my wrist." He lifted his arm, pulling up his sleeve.

Jarrett responded with a scoff. "A bright red string tie like Matt McCall used to wear."

Farley shifted a toothpick from one side of his mouth to the other. "Looks like McCall's boy is tryin' to copy his old man."

"I think we should be cautious about reaching any such conclusion," Stacey proclaimed. "What happened to Bo last night had a very theatrical quality to it. Matt McCall's medicine show shenanigans were, in all likelihood, a product of desperation. But last night was carefully staged for motivations which remain unknown. The announcement that Matt McCall's son lives in Travis and has been waiting to wreak vengeance on his father's killer could well be a ploy."

Rance noted an air of confusion in the room and decided to elaborate. "I agree with Stacey. The notion that McCall has a son living in Travis, who suddenly decides to go after the man that took down his father more than twenty years ago, well . . ."

"Guess we need to study on it some," Farley conceded.

Jarrett slapped his desk. "Gents, we've said about all there is to say right now. Let's grab some dinner. We don't want to be late for the meeting at the town hall."

"What meeting?" Bo asked.

"You surely have been sleepin', Preacher," Farley gleefully informed. "Why, there's flyers hangin' on ever' post in town. The Conrad Western Railroad is havin' a big meetin' tonight, but it ain't 'bout politics."

Thad once again spoke directly to the pastor. "Cassie told me the meeting is important and it isn't about the referendum. She really wants me there and . . ." the sheriff made a nervous gesture with his hands. "You know how that daughter of mine can be."

A sense of unease filled the room. Dehner shattered it. "Let's get out of here and chow down. Like the sheriff said, we don't want to be late."

One hundred chairs filled the town hall. An aisle ran down the center, leaving an even fifty chairs on each side.

In one of the first rows sat Cassie Jarrett, with Farley Canton on her left side, her father on the right.

Bo Jefferson stood in the back along with Rance and Stacey. They were there to help quell any violent outbursts. The pastor would attempt sweet reason. Rance and Stacey were on hand in case the reason turned sour.

The pastor looked around him as the crowd

entered the hall at a steady trickle. "We have a small drama here pointing to a larger problem," he observed in a whisper to Dehner and Hooper. "Folks opposing the railroad are sitting on one side, people supporting the referendum are on the other. Those in favor of the railroad are sitting on the same side as Cassie. Everyone knows Cassie is a big proponent of the railroad. The situation is going to make Thad uneasy."

"There's another drama being played out here," Stacey added. "One of a more universal nature. Poor Farley Canton is obviously in love with the boss' daughter. He keeps trying to engage Miss Jarrett in conversation, but the lady does little more than nod her head."

Jefferson smiled sadly. "I'm afraid Farley's situation is hopeless. The man in Cassie's life is sitting up front behind the podium, Mayor Reade Bourke. He and Cassie are sort of engaged, though there has been no formal announcement."

Dehner asked an obvious question. "How does Thad feel about his daughter's 'sort of' engagement?"

Bo Jefferson went quiet. He watched the increasing number of people who were entering the building. Some folks would have to remain on their feet. One hundred chairs were not enough.

"I've known Thad Jarrett for a long time," he finally answered. "We know a lot about each other. But there are matters Thad keeps locked up inside. Cassie fits into that category."

All the chairs were now filled, and people were lining the back and side walls. Mayor Reade Bourke made his way to the podium. He was a tall, barrel-chested man with a square, deeply tanned face. His brown uncombed hair formed a ragged line over his ears.

While he looked comfortable in his expensive suit, Bourke's appearance was rugged. Dehner reckoned Reade Bourke was an exception in at least two ways, to most mayors found in western towns. Still shy of twenty-five, Bourke was a rancher, not a store owner or a banker.

"Time to get started, folks!" Bourke's voice was friendly, but it carried the undertone of an order. "This is a special meetin'. As you can see, there are two gents sittin' behind me. One is Mr. Kain Arnell of the Conrad Western Railroad. All of you know the other jasper: Riley Bennett, the editor, reporter, and typesetter for the *Travis Gazette*."

There was a scattering of applause, which Bourke talked over. "Kain Arnell has somethin' he wants to say, so I'll sit down and let him say it."

Kain nodded at Bourke as he approached the podium. "Thank you, Mr. Mayor, and thank you all for coming. I'm going to ask for a quick show of hands. How many of you read *The Saturday Evening Post*?"

There was a moment of confused silence. Nobody had anticipated the question. Eventually about half of the assembled raised their hand.

"I'll bet many of you have seen the advertisements in that magazine for the Conrad Western Railroad. The ads that read at the top, 'The Facts from the Tracks.' That's a clever phrase, someone smarter than me thought it up."

There were a few polite chuckles. People still couldn't fathom where this was leading.

"I may not be great at writing slogans," Kain continued, "but I can come up with a few good notions of my own. Recently, I got in touch with the *Post* staff in Philadelphia. I suggested an article commemorating the twenty-second Anniversary of the shootout between Thad Jarrett and Music Matt McCall. They loved the idea!"

A few gasps and stirrings of excitement came from the crowd. Energized by the positive response, Arnell spoke louder. "The Conrad Western Railroad greatly admires the pioneers of Travis, Arizona and we want your town to receive the recognition it deserves no matter how you vote on the referendum!"

Cheers and applause exploded in the town hall. Several elderly people cupped hands over their ears to muzzle the racket.

Kain Arnell stood at the podium enjoying his triumph. When the noise began to diminish, he waved his arms, pretending he wanted the crowd to become silent. "This project is now in the hands of the people of Travis. To tell you more, here as Mayor Bourke said, is a man you all know. The editor of Travis' great newspaper, Riley Bennett!"

The stirring introduction brought applause, though with lowered enthusiasm. Riley Bennett didn't naturally engender excitement. He was gaunt, in his early thirties, with hair an odd shade of yellow, probably the result of a childhood illness. Wire rimmed spectacles rested on his nose and often on the top of his head. By necessity a strap was attached to the spectacles, the only way to assure Riley wouldn't lose them.

The *Travis Gazette* occupied all of Riley's life, a situation that seemed to make him happy. In fact, Riley often appeared amused by some fallacy in the universe only he could spot.

"The staff of *The Saturday Evening Post* have left this project entirely in my hands," Riley declared with obvious glee. "I plan to take pictures in Snake Creek where the shootout took place. Of course, Snake Creek is a ghost town now. Anybody with sense left that place years ago for Travis."

Riley laughed hard at this own joke, then explained further. "I took a look see at Snake Creek this morning and most of the buildings involved in the shootout are still standing. I plan to restage the gunfight. Take pictures using Thad

Jarrett and Bo Jefferson. 'Course, I'll have to get some other gents to be McCall and the jasper on the roof. I haven't been able to locate those two."

Bennett laughed again, this time many in the crowd laughed with him.

"The *Post* doesn't plan to print the story until late next month. That's well after the vote, which is next Tuesday, one week from now. So I know Reverend Jefferson and Sheriff Jarrett will be happy to go along. After all, we'll be doing all this on a Saturday. The town council has declared the day to be a festival day. There will be games for the children. Everybody come and bring a picnic basket!"

Loud cheers once again resounded across the room. "Dear God," Jefferson said in a low voice. It sounded almost like a prayer.

Dehner looked toward the front row. A lot of motion was coming from both Thad Jarrett and Cassie. Rance surmised that the sheriff and his daughter were having an argument conducted in whispers.

Riley waved at the crowd and sat down as the thunder began to subside. Reade Bourke quickly returned to the podium. "Reckon I should apologize to Sheriff Jarrett and Reverend Jefferson for not giving them a warning about our plans. The secrecy was my idea. You see, I know Bo and Thad pretty darn well. They are humble men who both think there has been too much fuss about the killing of Matt McCall. Well, I say these two gentlemen deserve a lot of credit and we're going to see that they get it, this Saturday! This meeting is done. Good night!"

Whoops followed as people ambled out of the hall, discussing the upcoming festivities. Bo Jefferson put on a mask of politeness as folks gathered around him.

Thad Jarrett couldn't manage that. He quickly departed from the town hall, silent and grim faced.

Rance looked around for Cassie. She was huddled in a corner with Reade Bourke. They also looked grim.

CHAPTER TEN

Thad Jarrett watched as Ezra Smith, owner of the Dusty Trail Saloon, closed the double doors that fronted the bat wings and locked them. Turning from the doors, the saloon owner spotted Jarrett standing in the middle of the street.

"Evenin', Thad. Guess I should say, 'mornin' Thad.'"

"Yep. It's well past two. Go home and get some sleep, Ezra."

"Reckon I'll do jus' that."

Thad watched Ezra amble off, then continued his round, walking in the opposite direction of the saloon owner. The lawman tried to tell himself that this was an average night. Ezra closing up the Dusty Trail usually indicated most of the town was sleeping.

Jarrett suddenly stopped and angrily kicked a small stone. "Cassie had no business trapping me at the meeting," he declared to himself.

He walked on as his mind reviewed the events of only a few hours before. After the meeting ended, Cassie had pleaded, "You must do it, Father. The whole town will benefit from being in such an important magazine. *The Saturday Evening Post* was founded by Ben Franklin in . . ."

"I know who founded it!"

She took his hand and gently squeezed it. "Please Father. Maybe it shouldn't be, but this is important to me. Do it for your stubborn daughter."

Cassie hadn't spoken to him in such a sweet manner in years. Her words threw him off balance. "Okay."

"Wonderful. With you agreeing, I know Bo Jefferson will also go along. I'm going to tell Reade."

And she darted off. Having gained what she wanted with sweetness, she cast him aside and left him sitting there.

The lawman again spoke to himself. "My daughter fooled me like a carnival barker tricks a poor farm boy."

Thad continued his round, first approaching the office and home of Doctor Raikin. On his right, next door to the doc's residence was Murphy's Barber Shop, followed by the Travis Emporium. Across from the emporium was a store bearing the name Hardware. The owner reckoned that was enough.

There wasn't anything past those businesses except the schoolhouse about twenty yards away. The sheriff always included the school in his rounds. Travis had a slew of mischievous boys who loved pranks and, not surprisingly, the school was their frequent target.

A mountain shaped cloud momentarily blocked the moon. The lantern hanging from

Doc Raikin's house now provided the only light.

A voice suddenly resounded from the alley between the barber shop and emporium. *"When the trumpet of the Lord shall sound . . ."*

The sheriff halted his steps in front of the barber shop. From the other side of the emporium came: *"And time shall be no more . . ."*

Thad's eyes shifted to the other side of the street where a figure stepped out from the side of the hardware store, singing: *"And the morning breaks eternal bright . . ."*

The lawman spotted movement from the alley. He hit the ground as a red flame streaked over him. Lying flat, Jarrett returned fire.

Frantic sounds of running footsteps filled the air. Thad started to spring to his feet and begin pursuit, but was stopped when a flying object smashed against him. The sheriff once again collided with the ground. He tried to blink away the red splotches in front of his face. He had been jumped and the attacker was now on top of him.

Jarrett balled his fist but never threw a punch. His adversary appeared unconscious. Maybe the collision had knocked the man out, or maybe . . .

Footsteps sounded once again, but this time they were approaching. Blood dripped from the corpse Rance Dehner pulled off the sheriff.

"What happened?" Dehner asked.

"I'm trying to figure that out." Jarrett gave Dehner a quick summary of the events as he picked himself up. Both men then crouched over the dead body.

"This is Varn Tobin, the jasper I tangled with on my first day in Travis," Dehner said.

"There goes my idea of keeping an eye on Tobin and trying to find out who had hired him."

"The idea was good," Dehner assured. "But Stacey and I did a lousy job of carrying it out. We searched for Tobin all day and couldn't find him."

"The blood on his face is fresh, hitting me knocked several teeth out and cut his lip." The sheriff looked upward. "Someone tossed Tobin's dead body off the roof of Murphy's Barber Shop."

Dehner pointed at Tobin's neck. "He's been strangled. His killers didn't want a messy corpse. This theatrical production, complete with singing, has been carefully planned."

"It's been planned all right," Jarrett nodded toward the corpse's wrist. A red string tie was wrapped around it.

CHAPTER ELEVEN

Rance Dehner and Stacey Hooper sat in Jerry's Restaurant indulging in a second cup of coffee after finishing breakfast. The *Travis Gazette* lay on the table in front of them.

"The paper has all the details regarding Bo Jefferson's run in with the singing assailant and his accomplices, including the melodramatic claim that Matt McCall's son is a resident of Travis seeking blood vengeance for his father's death," Stacey observed.

"Yep," Rance added. "Billy not only got fifty cents out of Bo, I suspect he got even more from Riley Bennett for giving him that story."

Stacey smiled in agreement. "Billy no doubt enjoys many drinks as a result of his devotion to the public's right to know."

"Suppose so . . ." Rance stared at his empty plate for a moment. "I almost dread tomorrow's newspaper."

"I am shocked to hear you say such a thing," Stacey mockingly declared. "Surely you are aware of the obligation we all have to be informed citizens."

"Riley Bennett probably checks in with the undertaker daily," Dehner explained. "He'll learn about the strangled corpse, then run to Sheriff

Jarrett for details. Thad feels an obligation to be open with the press."

Dehner took a slow sip of coffee, then continued. "Bennett will spot the hook for his report. Bo was told that if Thad Jarrett didn't leave his office and the town, at first there would be a killing not all that close to him. Subsequent killings would get closer. The implication being Thad Jarrett's friends and family would suffer if he didn't leave."

"And Varn Tobin was the first step in that threat being realized."

"Looks that way, Stacey."

The breakfast hour was ending. The restaurant staff bustled around many of the surrounding tables retrieving dirty dishes. All the staff were Chinese. Dehner wondered, casually, if "Jerry" was an Americanization of a Chinese name.

His thoughts returned to more urgent matters. "Thad wants us to be at the rally that Link and Tracey Bonner are holding tonight to oppose the railroad."

"Sounds like the sheriff has made a very sound proposal."

"Maybe." Dehner took his final sip of coffee. "But we are dealing with an unpredictable enemy."

"I must agree. Any enemy that assaults the sheriff by tossing a corpse off the roof of a barber shop is, indeed, unpredictable."

"I ran into Link Bonner yesterday," Dehner informed. "He was at the emporium buying supplies. He and his wife are fixing up the school today. We need to keep watch on them."

Stacey, in turn, finished his coffee. "How do you propose to do that? The area around there is barren."

"But there are woods about fifteen yards behind the school."

"So, we shall be spending the day amongst the forested splendors of nature."

"Yes," Dehner said as both men rose from the table.

"I hate the forested splendors of nature," Stacey declared as the two men left the restaurant.

CHAPTER TWELVE

Stacey looked up at the sun, which indicated noon was approaching. He shifted his weight from one foot to the other. "Our five hours or so in these wretched woods have brought me to conclusions both practical and academic," Stacey whispered to his companion.

"What's your practical conclusion?" Dehner asked. He also spoke in a whisper.

"Travis is a town blessed with two dedicated educators. From what I can make out from studying the side window, Tracey is painting, and Link is pounding something with a hammer. They are obviously preparing for school reopening in the fall. No doubt, they will continue with their good deeds without pausing for lunch."

Rance grinned. "And your academic insight?"

"Those poets who proclaim the glories of nature have spent little time in it. Nature is an abundance of dirt, bugs, and thorns."

Dehner chuckled lightly at his friend's remark, then fell silent as a small buckboard pulled up in front of the school. He motioned for Hooper to follow him as he moved to the edge of the woods where they could get a better view of the wagon.

Two men sat on the bench of the wagon. They were both clothed in bib overalls. Large straw hats adorned their heads. The apparent farmers jumped off the wagon quickly and gracefully. These were not old men.

Link emerged from the schoolhouse. He shook hands with the men in a manner which suggested he was seeing them for the first time. After what seemed a friendly talk, Link motioned for them to follow him inside.

"The newcomers are probably recently arrived homesteaders," Stacey surmised. "Enterprising men of the soil who want to check out the educational opportunities being offered for their progeny by Travis, Arizona."

"I don't like this, Stacey. Look at the two horses hitched to the buckboard and the cayuse tied behind it."

"All very fine steeds."

"Exactly. Those horses haven't spent any time pulling a plow. We need to take a closer look."

As Dehner and Hooper stepped out of the woods, a scream blared from the school. Both men dashed toward the building. One of the straw hatted outlaws barged from the schoolhouse carrying Tracey over his shoulder. She was limp, her head bleeding.

The second straw hat emerged gun in hand. He looked quickly toward the town, checking for any trouble. Spotting none, he turned and saw the threat coming from the woods. Rance and Stacey hit the ground feeling heat from the bullets soaring directly over them.

Neither Dehner nor Hooper risked returning fire. Their enemies had a hostage. They watched as in blur of speed, Tracey was dumped into the back of the buckboard, the shooter untied and mounted the cayuse, and the other straw hat turned the wagon around and sped from town. The shooter rode behind him.

"I'll go after them," Rance's words collided as he and Stacey sprang onto their feet. "Help Link, he's probably hurt bad."

Dehner ran back into the woods towards a clearing where he and Hooper had tied their horses. He rode his bay out of the trees and brush in time to spot a distant cloud of dust coming from the flat road.

The bay was rested and ready for a fast gallop. The horse quickly ate up ground. As the dust cloud drew nearer, Dehner saw the shooter glancing backwards, gauging his adversary's progress.

The detective's mind frantically considered a course of action. The outlaws only needed a few seconds to kill Tracey Bonner. He had to be mindful of the woman's plight. But he couldn't allow the kidnappers to vanish with Tracey.

Moments later, the outlaws surprised and confused him. They reached a fork in the road. The shooter rode off onto the side path while the driver of the buckboard remained on the main road, which swerved into a curve up ahead.

"They could be setting up a trap," Dehner said aloud.

Rance continued to make huge gains on the buckboard. From what he could see, the two horses pulling the contraption were tiring.

The wagon followed the curve in the road where a large and sprawling hill blocked the buckboard from view. A sharp cracking sound suddenly cut the air, followed by a man's yell.

Dehner pulled up the bay before going around the curve. The wagon had apparently broken down.

Apparently.

This could be a ploy, but Dehner's instincts told him otherwise. He decided to test them out. Dismounting, he grabbed the reins of his bay. Rance pointed it at the hill and gave the animal a hard slap. The horse galloped up the hill, hoofbeats thundering on the ground.

Dehner drew his Colt. Quickly and quietly, he moved around the curve. The buckboard was tilted sideways. The boards on the wagon blocked his view of Tracey.

But Straw Hat was standing beside the broken wagon, gun drawn and looking up in the direction of the hoofbeats. A look of alarm creased his face. He saw that the horse was riderless.

"Drop the gun!" Dehner shouted the command.

Straw Hat had no intention of obeying. He swung his gun in Rance's direction. Dehner pumped a bullet into the man's chest, causing him to yell once again as he was propelled backwards.

The detective could take no chances. Tracey was still in easy range of her kidnapper's weapon. Dehner sent two more red flames into Straw Hat's chest.

The outlaw jerked violently and dropped to the ground.

Rance ran to his victim. Satisfied that the kidnapper was dead, he hurried to the bed of the wagon and helped Tracey to sit upright.

"Thank you . . . Rance . . ." the woman coughed as she spoke, one hand was pressed against her head.

"Take it easy, Tracey, you'll be back in Travis soon, we'll . . ."

The woman cut him off with a frantic question. "How is Link?"

"He's just fine."

Dehner hoped he was telling the truth.

CHAPTER THIRTEEN

Link Bonner wasn't exactly fine, but he was doing okay for a man who had been stabbed. Stacey Hooper had managed to stop the bleeding and get Link to the doctor in quick time. Tracey's head injury required a bandage but was not serious.

The "Vote No Meeting" at the town hall was packed that night. Link appeared wan but happy as he stood at the front looking over the eighty or so people. "We've never managed a large crowd like this before," he proclaimed to Rance and Stacey.

"You have Riley Bennett to thank," Dehner explained. "Riley wrote up an account of what happened to you and Tracey this afternoon and posted it in the window of the *Travis Gazette*. You are now what is known in show business as a star."

Stacey shook his head in mock solemnity. "But remember, stardom is fleeting, especially for schoolteachers."

Rance and Stacey left the front of the town hall and each positioned himself on one side of the room where they could keep watch for any trouble. Thad Jarrett was stationed in the back while Farley Canton patrolled outside.

Rance's observation about the celebrity status

of Link and Tracey Bonner proved accurate. For most of the meeting, the couple fielded questions about the attack they had experienced a few hours before. Tracey and Link both tried to move the conversation onto the upcoming referendum.

Their success was minimal. At one point, under the guise of asking a question, a man managed to rise and in a slurred voice declared, "That whole kidnak thing is bullfeathers. You're tryin' to give the railroad a bad name."

Standing nearby, Stacey Hooper responded, "Sir, men like you give the civilized practice of enjoying a fine beverage a bad name." He escorted the drunk out to the sounds of laughter.

"That's about as good as it is going to get tonight," Link whispered to his wife, who nodded her bandaged head in agreement.

Link thanked the crowd and ended the meeting.

Riley Bennett hurried out of the town hall and began a fast walk to the office of the *Travis Gazette*. Riley was a man who rarely paused to glance back. The reporter was startled as he barged into his workplace and a voice boomed behind him, "Getting started on another long night, Riley?"

His body stiffened in surprise. Riley faced the man standing only a few feet behind him. "Ah, yes, Kain, the newspaper business demands long nights."

Kain Arnell closed the door behind him, approached Riley and gave him a wide smile. "Travis is fortunate to have a dedicated journalist like you serving the town."

There was something in that smile that made Riley nervous. "Ah, thanks."

Kain strolled further into the office and began to look around. "I suppose the big item for your next edition will be the whole story on the terrible ordeal Link and Tracey Bonner went through this afternoon."

Riley followed the railroad man, noting that at the present moment, Kain seemed more at home in the office than he did. Bennett tried to sound casual. "Of course, that will be the lead on the front page."

Arnell again faced the reporter. The intimidating smile was still there as he handed Riley a piece of paper. "This will be an enormous help with your article. It is a quote from Bradford Conrad, President of Conrad Western Railroad, expressing his deep regret for the incident this afternoon and his relief and joy that Link and Tracey Bonner are okay."

Riley examined the paper. "This is handwritten. Conrad couldn't possibly know about the attack unless you sent a tele—"

"I haven't wired Mister Conrad yet." Arnell's face turned serious as he put a heavy emphasis on the word, "mister." "But I have total authority to speak for him. You can print those words as if they came from Bradford Conrad himself."

Kain Arnell took on a mockingly thoughtful pose as he glanced at the ceiling. "In fact, I think it would be a great idea to give President Conrad's words a prominent place in your story. Somewhere in the first three paragraphs."

"Well—"

Kain stuck a finger into Riley's chest. "I'll bet you're looking forward to doing that article for *The Saturday Evening Post*."

Bennett almost raised his hands as if a gun were pressing against him. "Yes, but . . ."

Kain withdrew his finger. "Yep. Those folks in Philadelphia took my word that you could handle the assignment. I haven't had a reason to tell them any different. So far."

Arnell turned and walked toward the door. "I'll leave you alone, Newspaperman. You've got a lot of work to do."

Kain Arnell opened the door and before stepping out gave his victim another wide smile.

CHAPTER FOURTEEN

Stan Goodey, the owner of Goodey's Travelling Circus, stood in the middle of his circus' ring. A huge crowd surrounded him. Goodey was a grotesquely obese man. He yelled to the audience as he chewed on a cigar. Brown spittle shot from his mouth.

"Ladies and Gentlemen, boys and girls, I bring you the funniest sight on earth. Kain Arnell, the man with no legs!"

Arnell walked into the ring as the tent shook from mocking laughter. His torso sat on two large clown feet. He was, as Goodey proclaimed, the man with no legs.

Goodey laughed along with the paying customers. "I think we should give Kain a lift."

Smoke from Goodey's cigar formed a cloud around Kain and he was suddenly propelled upward onto a trapeze. But he immediately lost his balance and fell off.

Hitting the earth, Arnell realized his back was broken. Lying helpless on the ground, he could hear a creaking sound moving toward him. Terror shot through Arnell as a voice proclaimed as if from a pulpit, "You deserve it."

Kain recognized the voice, but he couldn't see

the man, only the rotating spokes of a gigantic wheelchair rolling toward him.

Arnell's eyes opened; the room surrounding him looked strange. Where was he?

The grogginess of sleep lifted. He inhaled deeply as reality replaced the nightmare. He was in Travis, Arizona doing a dirty job. But a job that paid good money, and just maybe, riches.

He glanced at the small window in his hotel room. A light tint of red formed a knife in the gray sky. Arnell got out of bed. He didn't want to return to sleep.

The mirror on the wall over the chest of drawers was cracked and smudged, but it would do. Arnell picked up the pitcher that rested on the small chest of drawers, poured water into a basin and began to shave using the blade and other instruments he had placed there the previous night before bedding down.

Kain Arnell always planned carefully in advance. At the age of fourteen, he had schemed for weeks on how he would run away with Goodey's Travelling Circus when it arrived at his small Indiana town.

Those three years he had spent with the circus were wonderful—until. At first, he had been assigned to smelly, unpleasant jobs nobody else wanted. He didn't mind. It was far better than doing farm chores and listening to his parents rag him whenever he tried for a little fun.

The circus people didn't care if he got drunk as long as it didn't interfere with his work. Hell, they even gave him booze and tobacco.

Arnell dunked his blade into the basin, then continued shaving. Duke Scott, the star of the circus, had pulled a fifteen-year-old kid out of cleaning animal cages and trained him to be a trick rider like himself.

"Kain, this circus has a bunch of clowns, three elephants, four monkeys, two lions and a family of trapeze artists. But only one trick rider, and kid, that is what most people come to see. You and me will work together most nights. But sometimes one of us will want a night off and when that night comes, the Goodey Travelling Circus will still have a trick rider."

The next few months were the hardest of his life. But with Duke's instructions and patient encouragement, he learned how to stand up on the saddle of a galloping horse. He even conquered the most difficult stunt of all. While holding on to the horn of his saddle, he would slide off and immediately press his legs together and hold himself against the side of the horse. The idea was that the horse was shielding him from any outlaws that might attack.

Arnell smirked as he scraped the last stubble off his face. He had needed to pull that stunt three times while riding around the circus ring, so everyone in the audience could see it. Each time he had to pull a gun from a holster he was wearing and fire blanks into the air.

Kain dropped the blade into the basin, spraying water drops onto the chest of drawers. He stared at his reflection in the mirror and that horrible night returned, as it frequently did.

Duke Scott was riding in front of him. Duke would perform the tricks first, then Kain would follow. Kain didn't see what went wrong but Duke fell from his steed. Kain tried to rein in his galloping horse, but the animal went up on its hind legs and came down on Scott.

Duke screeched in pain as Arnell's horse whinnied and began to wildly stomp about, kicking up sawdust. Screams and shouts came from the crowd. Two men ran to help the fallen rider and Stan Goodey quickly appeared. "Get him outta here," he motioned toward the open flap in the tent. Duke continued to contort in pain as he was hastily tossed over the saddle of his horse and the animal fast-walked out of the tent.

Kain watched in stunned horror, but the spell was quickly smashed by his boss' orders. "Start riding!"

"Wha—"

"You're paid to be a trick rider. Do your act!"

Kain Arnell calmed his horse, gave the animal a reassuring pat, and then followed the boss' orders. As he carried out his act, he could hear

Stan Goodey's voice booming from the center of the ring. "Nothin' to be worried 'bout, folks! Duke Scott is a tough cowpoke who lives on horses. He'll be back on his pinto soon. Meanwhile, cast your eyes on Duke's saddle partner as he performs breath takin' feats for your entertainment!"

Arnell began to dress as he shook his head at the naivete of his seventeen-year-old self. At the time, he had thought it fortunate that the accident happened on an opening night in Denver, Colorado. They would be in Denver for a week. The town had a good hospital. Duke would return in a few days, restored to his old self.

The reality was much harsher. Kain was attending to the two horses he and Duke employed in their act when he heard voices outside the tent.

"Scott's returned, ridin' in the back of a buggy, shoutin' out for help."

"Let him shout . . ."

The young man understood what he had just heard. Circus people were superstitious. They wouldn't go near a man who had been injured doing his act, not until that man had fully recovered.

Kain hurried from his tent. Locating the buggy was easy. He could hear the driver's angry complaint, "Look mister, I ain't paid ta help no cripple git his wheeler chair outta my cab and then have ta help the buzzard again ta . . ."

"Duke!"

"Kain!" The joy in his mentor's voice made the young man strangely uneasy. The uneasiness increased as he removed the wheelchair from the back of the buggy and then helped Duke Scott into it. His mentor now looked haggard and defeated.

Kain and Duke watched as the buggy driver slapped the reins of his horse, prodding it forward. Once the vehicle was safely out of hearing range, Duke spoke up. "Thanks, kid, you'd think that driver woulda' helped some," Scott's words were low and resentful. "I had to pay him enough for the ride."

Kain's uneasiness began to morph into terror. The man he had looked up to and considered to be his real father was now a pitiful shell. "Don't let that driver worry you none, Duke. Jus' think about getting out of that crazy contraption you're sitting in and getting back on your horse. Why, we'll be riding—"

"Could you push me to Mr. Goodey's tent?"

"Ah, sure."

Everyone in the circus knew Stan Goodey didn't like to be approached by the hired help. As he proclaimed frequently, "I'll come to you when I need you. Meanwhile, don't never bother me."

But surely, this would be an exception, Arnell thought to himself. After all, Duke Scott was the star of the circus. Featured prominently outside the main tent was a big drawing of Duke, standing up on his pinto, firing a gun.

Kain knew he had been wrong the moment he wheeled his mentor into Stan Goodey's tent. Goodey was seated at a battered table shuffling papers. At first, he looked up in shock at the people who had entered his domain without permission. The shock became contempt. "What is it?"

"I'm real sorry to bother you Mr. Goodey, but I need to talk about something urgent."

To Kain Arnell, Scott's voice sounded all wrong. He was used to hearing his mentor come across as a man in charge. Now the man who was featured in splendor in that well displayed drawing sounded humble and contrite.

"I'll never ride again, Mr. Goodey. But I can still be of value to the circus. I got a real head for business. Back in school, arithmetic was my best subject. Why—"

Goodey cut in. His voice didn't contain a trace of emotion, making it even more frightening. "Today is Thursday. The circus leaves town after two performances on Saturday. I'll give you food and lodging 'til then. After that, you're on your own."

"But, Mr. Goodey, my legs are no good but I can—"

"You're of no use to me. Get out or I'll have you thrown off the property."

Kain quickly pushed the wheelchair out of the tent. He couldn't stand to see Duke Scott grovel.

The young man continued to push the wheelchair along the stony ground the circus was camped on as he babbled nonsense about Duke's legs being restored in a day or two. Emotionally exhausted, he stopped under a scraggly tree which offered a touch of shade from the July sun.

Scott finally spoke up, his voice resounding with a new confidence. "To hell with Goodey's Travelling Circus!"

Kain was elated that his mentor no longer talked like a broken man. "That's right, Duke, to hell with it!"

"Circus life is okay, but only for a while. Know what we gotta do, kid?"

Duke answered his own question. "We should start a horse ranch! Now, you'd have to do the work, kid. The physical work, I mean. But I know horses and I know business. We'd make a great team. Why, in a year or two, we'll be rich! We'll use hired hands for the work. What do you say?!"

Staring into the face of his mentor, Arnell realized he had mistaken desperation for confidence. Fear dominated Scott's eyes and his face contorted. He appeared to be on the verge of crying.

"Sure, Duke, sounds like a great idea!"

Arnell spent the rest of the day and the evening

encouraging Duke Scott in his fantasy. They would start the ranch right there in Colorado, not too far from Denver where Duke could get the very best medical attention. The young man passionately claimed he was looking forward to starting the ranch. "The man who taught me how to be a trick rider will now teach me how to be a rancher."

Kain Arnell repeated that statement several times. It brought reassurance and happiness to his former mentor.

But it was a lie. Several hours before dawn the next day, while the circus people slept, Kain Arnell saddled the horse he had used in his act and rode off. He never saw Duke Scott again.

Now fully dressed, Arnell looked at himself in the mirror. "A man has to be hard and cruel while pretending to be everyone's friend," he whispered to himself.

Arnell left the hotel and headed for Jerry's Restaurant. He was the first customer of the day. An elegantly attractive waitress in her early teens came to his table the moment he sat down.

"Good morning, sweetheart, you are the most beautiful sight this man will see today."

The girl's face turned red, and she looked downward. Kain Arnell felt good. He was in charge, a man who could always get what he wanted.

CHAPTER FIFTEEN

Thad Jarrett stood with hands on hips behind his desk, facing Rance Dehner and Stacey Hooper. "You're right Rance, that outlaw you dispatched to hell yesterday was a hired killer. Even dead, he had the look. And those guns he had strapped on under the overalls proved the point."

Jarrett dropped his hands and began to pace the office. "But the buzzard wasn't working alone. And I think there are more accomplices involved here than just the one who got away yesterday. Someone has brought in a gang."

Dehner nodded agreement. "And you're at the center of whatever plan they have. They want to enforce this myth that Matt McCall's son is living in Travis and is out for your blood."

Thad looked toward the window by the front door. "Let's hope it is a myth."

"They are following the narrative those attackers gave to Pastor Jefferson," Stacey added. "Their first victim, Varn Tobin, was someone you cared about only because he might inadvertently lead us to the instigator of all this madness. The two schoolteachers are a different matter altogether."

"I hate to think who's next in line." The sheriff returned to his desk. "This is a hard egg to unscramble, but . . ." He paused, then continued. "A gang needs a place to hide out. If they hung around town long, they would become conspicuous. I have a notion as to where they might be, a notion, nothing more."

A light came into Dehner's eyes. "I think I know what you have in mind."

Jarrett smiled wistfully. "After the war between the states, silver was located right outside of Travis. Two mines opened up. Those were crazy times with lots of restless men around. Within a few years those mines were closed. The strike was nowhere near what some folks had thought."

Dehner didn't even try to keep the amusement out of his voice. "But those worthless mines haven't gone unused."

"That's where we found the killers you were after, Rance. Other outlaws have hidden out in that area. There are also some old shacks around there. That kidnapper who deserted his partner yesterday might have been heading for one of the mines or shacks."

"You gentlemen have inflamed a desire in me to visit this locale with such a vivid history."

Thad barked a laugh. "You'll get your wish right now, Stacey. Things are crazy in Travis. Farley and I'd better stay in town. Could you two poke around the mines? Be careful. If you find signs of a hideout, come back."

Dehner and Hooper agreed to the sheriff's

request. On their way to the livery to retrieve horses, Rance spoke to his companion. "I hope we find the gang Stacey, but that is only part of the job."

Hooper nodded his head. "Yes, outlaws do not act voluntarily. Someone is paying them." He sighed deeply. "Once again, it all comes down to filthy lucre."

CHAPTER SIXTEEN

A film of dust settled on the clothing of Rance and Stacey as they examined the inside of a dilapidated cabin. "This is what comes from disturbing the particles of history," Stacey complained as he brushed his coat. "Even the mouse droppings in this place look ancient. I say we follow the example of the rodents and flee this wretched place."

Outside, the two volunteer deputies paused, enjoying the brisk breeze which engulfed the mountain they were on. "We've just confirmed an important point."

Stacey continued to brush himself off. "Oh? Please elaborate."

Dehner looked at the two mines, then peered downward at three shacks and the scattering of trees and brush that lined the mountain about fifteen yards down from where they stood. "Thad was right. This place is ideal for a hideout. But we haven't found any evidence that a group of people have been up here lately. That means the outlaws have probably been tipped off to find shelter elsewhere."

Dehner and Hooper began a downward walk to where their horses were tied. Stacey's bad mood was beginning to dissipate. "The person who's paying these ruffians knows the lay of the land."

"Exactly," Rance affirmed as they moved close to the cottonwood where their horses were tethered. "The leader of all this mayhem knows how Thad and I shot it out with the Grange brothers here. So this would be a place we'd routinely check out."

A rustling sound came from a wide maze of bushes behind the cottonwood. The horses nickered and tossed their heads.

Rance and Stacey communicated with a fast glance. Dehner spoke casually as he patted his bay. "As soon as we get back to town, I'm putting on the feed bag, for my horse and myself."

"Agreed!" Hooper heartily replied. "I recommend we dine at . . ."

Rance broke into a run and plunged into the waist high bushes. A figure that had been in a crouch sprang up and swiftly wound like a snake through the maze. As he began pursuit, Dehner noted that the subject of the chase was carrying a rifle.

But the rifleman chose not to use his weapon. He slithered from the brush and began a fast run downward, swerving and jumping over rocks and scrubs in an apparent effort to cause his pursuer to fall.

Dehner caught up with the rifleman and tackled him. They both rolled down the mountain until they collided with a large boulder. Rance scrambled to his feet, drew his gun, and then holstered it. His adversary had lost his weapon somewhere in the roll.

Besides, the man who slowly staggered onto his feet looked more pathetic than dangerous. White hair lapped over his shoulders. A similar colored beard covered a face with terrified eyes. His wiry body bordered on frailty. One side of his head was partially bald and appeared to have collapsed inward.

"What's your name?" Dehner demanded.

"Wally." The fear in Wally's eyes ratcheted up as he took a few steps away from the detective, then stopped. Trusting the stranger seemed a wiser move than attempting another run.

"You have a last name?"

"It's Lang-somethin'. Mebbe Langson. Not sure. Ain't used it fer a spell."

Stacey arrived carrying Wally's rifle. Dehner nodded to his friend to return the weapon to its owner. "Obliged." The look on Wally's face was one of childlike gratitude.

Rance's voice became softer. "Why were you spying on us?"

"Gotta. Bad men come up here sometimes." He looked carefully at Dehner. "Ya were with Sheriff Jarrett 'while back. Ya helped him take down them three buzzards. Saved my life."

Dehner looked quizzical. "I don't follow you."

"The bad men hid out in one of the caves,"

Wally pointed upward. "Late at night, while they were sleepin' I stole this here rifle off one of their saddles. Took ammo from the saddle bags. Next mornin' I heard them shoutin'. They knew someone was livin' 'round here and took the gun. If they'd found me, I woulda' been dead."

Wally looked at the ground. When he glanced up, his eyes were watery. "I know stealin' is wrong. But all I was eatin' was what dead critters I could find. With a gun, I kin shoot me a coyote or even a rabbit now and ag'in."

Dehner sighed and used an index finger to push his hat back a couple of inches. "How did you come to know Sherriff Jarrett, Wally?"

"Long time ago, I decided to leave the mountain. Had a burro then, rode him inta town. The sheriff was kind. He got me a job at the livery. I liked it there."

Like Dehner, Stacey Hooper spoke in a soft, nonthreatening manner. "If you liked the job, why did you leave?"

"My daddy tole me ta go back."

Stacey's eyebrows lifted in curiosity. "So, your father was working these old mines, trying to find silver?"

"No. Daddy was dead." Wally looked toward the sky. "Daddy's voice comes into my head. Only him and me know what's happenin'."

A sly smile snaked across Wally's face. He was about to let his two new friends in on a secret.

"My momma and sister died a long time ago, from the fever. Daddy tole me we'd had a lotta bad luck. Now was the time for good luck. So, we headed for these hills to find treasure."

Dehner resumed the questioning. "What happened to your daddy?"

"We was diggin' way back in one of the mines when there was sorta' a cave in. I got hit bad. Blacked out. When I woke up, Daddy was lyin' there dead. I thought I was gonna die too. I lay beside my Daddy for days, but I didn't die. That's when I went inta town. But Daddy's voice came inta my head and called me back. My luck is gonna change. I'll find treasure."

Rance looked away for a moment. He was facing a human tragedy. But a tragedy he could do nothing about. He felt wrong trying to get information from this man who was wounded in every way, but still tried. "Wally, did anybody come by here yesterday?"

"Yeh. A jasper ridin' his horse hard. He only came up the mountain part ways. He took his horse to the stream, then got him behind a big stone and jus' watched. I could tell the jasper was tryin' ta see if anyone was after him."

Dehner pressed on. "What happened next?"

Wally shrugged his shoulders. "Nothin'. After 'while, he rode off, away from town, that's all I can tell ya."

"Thanks Wally," Dehner said. "We'll leave you

to your mountain. I hope no more bad men bother you."

"Obliged. Daddy's voice gets easier to hear all the time. We're gonna find treasure real soon." He nodded goodbye and headed toward one of the mines.

Rance turned to his companion. "What do you think?"

Stacey Hooper looked at the retreating figure. "A man alone with only a voice in his head. May that voice always speak happy words."

CHAPTER SEVENTEEN

Farley Canton felt apprehensive as he dutifully carried out his early afternoon round. Several yards in front of him, walking in the same direction, was Cassie Jarrett. Viewing the lady as she gracefully made her way down the boardwalk accounted for the deputy's edgy state.

Farley was both smitten by Cassie Jarrett and hammered by reality. "Reckon Cassie and Reade Bourke is made for each other," he whispered. "They're both wealthy ranchers."

But silently Farley surmised he was by far a better man than Reade Bourke. Bourke was puffed up and full of himself, while . . .

Riley Bennett was walking toward Cassie. The newspaperman stopped in front of the young lady and began asking a load of questions. Cassie tried unsuccessfully to brush the reporter off, but Riley persisted.

"Bennett has no right to block a person like that," Farley was again whispering to himself. "The law needs to take action."

The lawman quickened his pace and could hear Cassie and Bennett arguing as he approached.

"Riley, I've already given you an interview."

"But so much has happened—"

"No."

"Just answer me this; your father has an excellent reputation with homesteaders. That reputation has spilled over onto the Circle J. Will you be talking with homesteaders about the upcoming referendum?"

"I never see any of the nesters! They aren't about to listen to a stranger!"

"But the opinion of Thad Jarrett's daughter—"

"That's enough, Bennett, move on!"

Riley appeared genuinely shocked as he turned and noticed the deputy. "Farley, what are you talking about?"

Farley tried to convey strong authority. "You're blockin' the boardwalk. And besides that, you're preventin' an innocent citizen from . . . ah . . . goin' 'bout doin' innocent stuff."

Riley shot back in kind. "Freedom of the press allows me to—"

"Perhaps two volunteer deputies can be of help here." The voice belonged to Rance Dehner, who casually approached the group, accompanied by Stacey Hooper. Stacey beamed a mischievous smile. He knew this was going to be fun.

Farley slid his thumbs into his gun belt, trying to appear as a man in control of the situation. "I thought you gents was checkin' out the territory 'round the old mines."

Stacey replied with gusto. "We have just returned from that strategic assignment."

As always, Stacey's words and demeanor left

Farley speechless. Rance took advantage of the silence. "Miss Jarrett, Stacey and I are heading for lunch at Jerry's Restaurant. Won't you please join us?"

"Why yes, I'd love to."

The two volunteer deputies departed with the young lady. With the reason for their argument gone, Farley and the reporter exchanged harsh stares and went their separate ways.

Cassie Jarrett chuckled lightly as they walked toward the restaurant. "Mr. Dehner and Mr. Hooper, I owe you. Thanks for pulling me out of that quicksand. I don't understand what it was all about."

Rance did understand but moved on to another matter. "Riley Bennett had a point about the homesteaders. As the boss of the Circle J, you may have some influence over the farmers."

Cassie shook her head. "I wasn't kidding with what I told Riley. I never see those people. The border area between the Circle J and the nesters isn't producing grass anymore. We can't use it. I am reading up on some studies being done on grazing land. More caution is needed in terms of grazing cattle."

Stacey Hooper held the door open as they entered Jerry's Restaurant. Cassie's appearance created a surge of excitement among the restaurant's staff. An Asian girl, one of the three daughters of the family that owned Jerry's, almost ran to Cassie and her companions and led them to a table.

Once they were seated, ordering required little thought. Beef stew was the only item available for lunch. Before the waitress hurried back to the kitchen, Cassie rewarded her with a "Thank you, Susie, you bring great honor to your family's establishment."

Stacey watched the girl hurry off. "We must dine with you more often, Miss Jarrett. You receive very special treatment."

Both Stacey and Rance were surprised by Cassie's reaction. A cloud of sadness enveloped her. She sighed deeply before speaking in a near whisper. "As always, what is good about the Jarrett family comes from my father. Years ago, he rescued the Wong family from thugs who didn't take to the Chinese. Father used money from the ranch to loan the Wongs what they needed to start this restaurant. They paid us back within a year."

Cassie Jarrett fell silent for a moment, and then the cloud dissipated. "Before we go any further, gents, I want us to be on a first name basis. Thad Jarrett considers you friends and so do I."

"Thank you, Cassie," Rance's smile indicated he and Stacey had been complimented. "What brings you into town today?"

Rance had intended the question to be casual. But the young woman pressed her lips together and looked downward before answering. "I haven't been much of a daughter lately. I'm here to drag Father back to the ranch for supper tonight. We need time together. I've been mad at Father because he won't support the railroad referendum. But of course, he shouldn't. After all, he and Bo are supervising the vote. And then . . ."

Susie returned carrying three large bowls on a tray along with napkins and utensils. She placed all the items carefully in front of her customers. All three diners tasted the stew and were vociferous in their compliments. Susie departed with a look of genuine joy on her face.

They ate in silence for a few minutes before Stacey returned to the point. "You were saying, 'and then,' Cassie. Was that a reference to the situation regarding *The Saturday Evening Post*?"

The lady sighed and nodded her head. "I knew Thad Jarrett would never go along with the notion of a restaging of his gunfight with Music Matt McCall. I put him in a situation where he almost had to say yes. That was wrong."

Cassie Jarrett stirred her stew. Anger laced her voice. "But the *Post* is a major magazine. The article could be a real boon to this town. Times are changing, Father needs to realize that!"

The lady took a deep breath and shook her head. "There I go again."

Deputy Canton's footsteps on the boardwalk blended with the hooting of an owl. At three AM, those were the dominant sounds in Travis.

Not that Farley Canton was paying any attention to sounds. He was still fretting over the incident that had occurred fifteen hours before.

"Made a damn fool of myself," he spoke in a normal voice. The owl being the only living thing nearby. "Shoulda' knowed a fancy gal like Cassie Jarrett might be nice and polite like to an ordinary fella, but she . . ."

Farley suddenly stopped. He thought he heard a voice coming from somewhere near the edge of town. "And it weren't no owl," this time, he whispered his words.

"When the trumpet of the Lord shall sound . . ."

"That's coming from the schoolhouse," he continued to whisper to himself.

The lawman's first thoughts went to the mischievous boys who frequently painted silly faces on the building they despised. All the crazy newspaper articles and town gossip could have them playing a different trick. But the singing voice didn't sound like a kid's. Still, Farley mused silently, some of those boys did have deep voices.

He hastened off what was left of the boardwalk and stepped quickly in the direction of the school.

"And time shall be no more..."

Thoughts twirled around in Canton's mind. This may not be a gag pulled by schoolboys.

Something far more dangerous could be going on here. Rance Dehner was dozing on the cot back at the office. Maybe he should get him. This could be a two man job.

Farley immediately rejected the notion. Whoever was hanging around the schoolhouse would take off when he saw the deputy running to get help.

Besides, Canton silently admitted to himself, he almost hoped there was a killer lying in wait for him. The deputy knew he could bring the outlaw in. He was every bit the lawman Thad Jarrett was, even though no one else knew it.

"And the morning breaks eternal bright and fair..."

The renewed singing purged all random thoughts from the deputy's mind. He cautiously approached the front door of the school and tried to open it. The door was locked, as it always was, against the young trouble makers.

Farley peered through the school's front window. Darkness peered back.

"When the saved of earth shall gather over on the other shore..."

Canton palmed his six shooter and crept around to the side of the schoolhouse where the singing seemed to be coming from. At first, he spotted nothing unusual, then from the far end of the school, a figure stepped into the metallic moonlight.

"Put your hands up, mister," Farley ordered. "I'm takin' you in."

The figure barked a laugh as he raised his hands. "Why are you taking me in, Deputy? Is it against the law to sing hymns early in the morning?"

Canton nervously stepped toward the man he wanted to make his prisoner. "No. But I'm taking you in fer questionin'."

This time, the laugh was louder and mocking. "You mean, you can't ask me questions right here?"

Farley now had a clearer view of his suspect. "When a fella's wearin' a black hood over his head, I think the sheriff's office is a right good place for questions. Now, real slow like take your gun out of the holster and drop it to the ground."

"Aren't you getting paid for unarming suspects, Deputy Canton? Or are you afraid to get close enough to me to take my gun? I'll bet Thad Jarrett wouldn't be afraid to do his duty and unarm a suspect."

A crippling swarm of emotions flooded over the young lawman. "I ain't afraid of you! Keep your hands high."

"Gladly."

Farley moved within a few feet of the suspect. He focused only on the gun he was to lift from its holster. He never noticed the black gloves on his suspect's hands or the fact that one of those hands was closed into a fist.

From the corner of his eye, Canton saw something swoosh in front of him like an attacking bird. Sharp pain seared his entire body. He heard his gun clatter on a stone. A second stab rendered his legs useless. He stumbled and hit the side of the schoolhouse.

For a horrifying moment, Farley Canton realized how easily he had been tricked. "Made a damn fool of myself," he said for a second time.

Those were the last words he ever spoke.

CHAPTER EIGHTEEN

Thad Jarrett felt odd as he poured himself a cup of coffee. Of course, he made coffee every day at the office, but he couldn't remember the last time he had done it in the kitchen of his own home.

A sense of wistfulness came over him as he carried the coffee to a small table located in the kitchen. Bo Jefferson had once declared half-jokingly that the sheriff's office was Thad's real home, not the Circle J.

Bo may have been right, Jarrett mused as he sat at the table. His mind drifted to the long friendship he had maintained with the pastor. A sad but persistent question pricked his mind. Samantha Preston had been the love of Bo's life. But the lady didn't love him back. At least not enough to live the life of a preacher's wife in a small western town.

Being rejected by Samantha had hurt Bo deeply. Cassie looked like Samantha, and the sheriff could spot sadness in Bo's eyes occasionally when he looked at Cassie.

"Bo often thinks about what he lost," Jarrett said to the bobbing liquid in his cup.

Then that pesky question returned. Thad wondered if Bo Jefferson had ever . . . known a woman, in the way the good book means it. After

Samantha left town, Bo showed no interest in any other lady. At that time, there hadn't been too many unmarried ladies in Travis to take an interest in. And Thad couldn't imagine his friend employing the services of a dove.

Bo Jefferson was Thad's best friend and frequent comrade in arms when violence needed to be quelled. Over the years, the two men had talked about every subject under the sun. Well, almost every subject.

Thad once again addressed his coffee cup. "I shouldn't even think about it. It's none of my business."

The kitchen door swung open, and Cassie walked in. Thad hoped she hadn't heard him talking to himself.

Apparently, she hadn't. "My goodness, you are ambitious this morning! You're up and dressed before four AM. The cook is probably just getting out of bed."

Thad waved an arm casually. "I want to get back to Travis early. I've made some coffee. Help yourself."

"I'll do just that." Cassie was in a robe and slippers. As she poured herself a cup of coffee and sat down with it at the table, she looked like a child. At least, she looked that way to her father.

"Whatcha been thinkin' about?" The woman's voice was playful.

Thad wanted to be honest, but not too honest.

"Oh, I've been thinking about Bo and how great it is to have a good friend at a time like this."

The playfulness left Cassie's voice. "You both oppose the railroad, right?"

Thad nodded. "But we try hard not to show it."

"Does it bother you that I am so open in supporting the referendum?"

The sheriff chuckled his reply. "Your mother and I gave up trying to keep strings on your tongue around the time you lost interest in rag dolls."

The woman sipped her coffee, then spoke in a low, apologetic manner. "I was wrong to set you up at that meeting about *The Saturday Evening Post*. But Father, practically the whole country reads the *Post*. The article will be a great benefit to Travis."

"Maybe so. And I confess, a railroad might help—"

Gunshots and loud whoops sounded from outside the ranch house. "Stay here," Thad snapped at his daughter as he sprang from his chair and darted toward the danger.

He stopped at the front door and drew his gun from the holster hanging on the hat rack. "Hey, inside the house, git outta yore beds and come see the present we left for ya!"

More gunfire followed. The thugs were firing into the air. They obviously thought their target had been caught by surprise.

"My turn to pull a surprise," the sheriff murmured as he flung open the door.

There were four hooded invaders on horseback. Lightning seemed to strike their bodies as they saw the armed lawman.

Thad fired. One of the outlaws screamed and jackknifed over onto his horse's neck.

Leaving the door open, Thad did a quick turn back into the house before a barrage of shots whizzed through the doorway.

Jarrett glanced sideways at the front window. "They'll be expecting me to come at them from the window." He spoke before a hail of bullets shattered the glass and proved him right.

Thad did a half twirl back to the doorway and again fired at the hooded riders. Only two of the outlaws were now in easy view. The shot missed them but deadened their will to fight. Behind the nearby shooters, Thad could see the injured man clinging to his horse as he galloped off. Another outlaw rode beside him.

The nearby thugs now turned and spurred their horses. The animals responded with a burst of speed and began a stampede into darkness.

Crouching low, Thad Jarrett ran after the outlaws. Confident he was close enough for a shot, the lawman hit the ground and fired. He cursed under his breath as his shot once again missed; not enough light to spot a likely target. But one of the riders returned fire. Thad was about to send a bullet in the direction of the red flame when he heard Cassie scream.

The lawman buoyed onto his feet and dashed toward his daughter. From the dark outline she cut against the night, Thad could see that Cassie was on her knees. As he got closer, he heard her crying.

The woman was looking down on a corpse. "Father, it's Farley Canton."

Thad crouched over the body of his deputy. Anger and sorrow laced his voice. "Farley was stabbed by someone who knew . . ."

He stopped speaking as his daughter rose to her feet and took several steps away. Cassie was trying, unsuccessfully, to stifle her emotions.

The sheriff went to his daughter and placed a hand on each of her shoulders. She spoke to him in a broken voice. "Farley loved me. I treated it like a joke. I didn't mean to be cruel. Farley was nice, but . . . you know . . ."

"Yes, I know."

"I always planned to have a talk with Farley, let him know that he was a good man who'd make some woman happy; now it's too late." The sheriff embraced his daughter as she cried into his shoulder. For the first time in a long while, Thad Jarrett felt close to his daughter. Cassie was childlike in her grief. He flashed back to the times when she really was a child, and the times when she had really needed him.

A scrambling sound caused the sheriff to look sideways to where several men were running toward him. The bunkhouse was a good distance from the ranch house, but the hands had obviously heard the shots.

Thad slowly broke the embrace and talked to his daughter as she saw the men approaching. "Cassie, I'm going to have a few of the hands help me, ah, place Farley's body in a buckwagon. They can take him into Travis."

"I'm going with them!"

"Fine. When you get to town, could you do me a favor?"

"Yes, what do you need?" Cassie's voice sounded anxious. She wanted desperately to do something meaningful.

"Tell Rance and Stacey what happened and tell them I've gone after the outlaws. They'll have to look after the town."

The woman now sounded hopeful. "Do you think you can catch them?"

"Maybe. The sun rises early this time of year. As soon as it gets light, I'm heading out to pick up their trail."

"You find those bad men, Father. And kill every one of them."

Thad Jarrett rode cautiously, eyeing the hill country around him. He wasn't surprised that the trail of the outlaws had led him to this area of the abandoned mines. But if the outlaws were up there, they had the advantage over him. He was ripe plucking for an ambush.

The lawman stopped and took out his field glasses. He couldn't spot anything unusual. He rode his chestnut up the largest hill, which contained the abandoned mines, as well as a stream which wound around it.

"A gang with a wounded man could find a stream to be very helpful," he informed his horse. He dismounted and ground tethered the animal, then slid the Winchester out of the scabbard of his saddle and proceeded on foot.

As Thad approached the water, he spotted a black circle moving in the sky. "Buzzards are circling something. Could be a dead animal."

But his instincts told him otherwise.

A shot fired and one of the buzzards dropped to the earth. A loud whoop followed. Thad immediately recognized the voice. Remaining vigilant, he made his way to the familiar figure who was now dancing about a dead bird as he waved his rifle in the air.

"Hello, Wally."

"Greetin's Sheriff. Been expectin' ya."

Jarrett immediately saw why he had been expected. For the second time that morning, he crouched over a corpse. This one had been shot twice. Once in the stomach and once in the chest.

"Know him, Sheriff?"

"No. But he has the look of a hardcase. I'm the one who gut shot him. Someone else put a bullet in his chest and sent him to hell. The second shot could have gone directly into his face, but whoever did it didn't think that necessary."

Wally shrugged his shoulders. "I don't foller ya."

"There's a gang operating in this area," Thad explained as he rose to his feet. "They're all outsiders." He pointed to the corpse. "It didn't make any difference to the gang if I recognized that jasper or not."

"I see yer point. But them bad men know all about this hill."

Jarrett nodded his head in agreement. "They know this is a great place to ride to when you want the law to lose your trail. An outlaw can take cover here for a while, but not too long. Other outlaws have hidden here. It's one of the first places I'd check for a hideout."

"If these bad men come from the outside, how'd they know all that?"

"Bad men don't work for nothing," Thad answered cynically. "A fine local citizen is paying them to kill." The lawman stopped talking and inhaled deeply. He couldn't allow his morose mood to take control. "Tell me what you saw here this morning."

Wally's attention had shifted to the sky. "Them buzzards flew off, but they didn't go far. They'll be making their way back soon." Returning his gaze to the earth, Wally saw the lawman now standing beside him looking impatient.

"Four men rode up ta the stream. One of them hurt bad. Guess they thought they could patch him up here while havin' a good look see if the law was comin'."

"Go on."

"Well, after a whiles I hear one of them say that the jasper you gut-shot wasn't gonna live. So, the fella doin' the talkin' pulls out his pistol. The jasper on the ground cries out like a kicked dog. Don't do no good."

"That's when he got shot in the chest."

"Yep. Then the shooter says, 'We'll leave him for the coyotes.' The other fellers didn't disagree none. They rode off." Wally paused as a fresh gleam came over him. "Say, I got a little proposition fer ya, Sheriff."

"Let's hear it."

"Ever' man's gotta right to a proper burial. I'll bury that feller in the ground if you'll allow me to keep his gun and gun belt. I only got me one box of ammo for this here rifle."

"It goes against my better judgment, but okay, Wally."

Wally gave another whoop. "Thanks, Sheriff. I'll put him in the ground in an hour or so after I git another chance at them buzzards. Workin' the mines sure puts an empty ache in a man's belly.

I've already killed me one buzzard. I'm gonna have a good breakfast."

Wally once again glanced at the sky and the winged darkness that was returning. "I'm gonna have me a good dinner, too."

CHAPTER NINETEEN

Thad Jarrett returned to Travis a quiet and withdrawn man. Dehner and Hooper understood the sheriff's emotions and only spoke to him when necessary. Thad had not been able to react to the death of his deputy. He had to repress his emotions as he pursued the killers of Farley Canton. Those repressed emotions were now surfacing.

At about mid-morning, Riley Bennett posted the news of Farley's death in the window of the *Travis Gazette*. Less than a half hour later, Kain Arnell entered the sheriff's office. Thad, Rance and Stacey all gave him polite but cold greetings.

Kain removed his hat. A look of mourning covered his face. "Sheriff Jarrett, speaking on behalf of the Conrad Western Railroad, I want to tell you how shocked and saddened we are by the brutal killing of your deputy."

Thad fidgeted in his desk chair, then managed a, "Thank you."

"The railroad wishes to see that Deputy Canton's widow receives some financial help at this time of tragedy and loss."

A note of anger now laced Jarrett's voice. "Deputy Canton wasn't married."

"Oh. Then perhaps he had family?"

"Farley Canton had no family," Dehner interjected. He wanted to save Thad Jarrett the irritation of dealing with a pest.

"Well . . . I assume there will be a service . . ."

"There will be a graveside service later this afternoon," Dehner informed. "The time will be posted in the *Gazette* office window soon."

Kain Arnell sensed the hostility in the room. "I'll see you gentlemen there." He returned his hat to his head and made a hasty exit.

Jarrett waved a fist in anger. "There goes a real . . ."

The lawman didn't finish the sentence. He didn't have to. Dehner and Hooper got the message.

There was a respectable attendance at Farley Canton's service. Bo Jefferson read the 23rd Psalm, then spoke his own words. "Farley Canton was a good deputy, and everyone agrees that someday he would have been an outstanding lawman. We mourn for what will not be.

"But Farley was a man who held no bitterness for his rough upbringing as an orphan. He endeavored to make Travis a better place, and in many ways, he made our lives a bit brighter. And so today we say thank you for a brief life well lived."

As Farley's coffin was lowered into the ground, Rance Dehner wondered how many funerals

Reverend Jefferson had to preside over for a person who had lived a "brief life."

Stacey Hooper had different thoughts. He posed a question as he and Rance walked back to the sheriff's office. "Did you notice the rather curious behavior of Cassie Jarrett and Reade Bourke?"

"What do you mean?"

"Cassie was standing between her father and Reade."

Dehner didn't doubt his friend had spotted something important. "I noticed that much, what did I miss?"

"At two points in the service, Reade tried to hold Cassie's hand. He obviously wanted to assert that they were there as a couple. Cassie resisted the gentleman's subtle advances. She even took a small step away from his honor the mayor, to be closer to her father."

"Very curious, but I don't know what to make of it." Dehner suddenly stopped on the boardwalk and pointed to an open doorway. "Speaking of curious, let's stop here and see if I've received a reply to my telegram."

The stop was less than a minute. They left the telegraph office disappointed.

Stacey understood the slowness. "I know your boss Bertram Lowrie is a fine man, but he is also a fine businessman. You are not conducting official business here in Travis. No doubt, Mr.

Lowrie admires your efforts on behalf of a living legend, but he must give highest priority to the cases his agency is being paid to conduct."

"Sure," came the reluctant reply. "But I'll hear from him soon, probably tomorrow."

Stacey smiled and said nothing.

The sun had set when Thad Jarrett returned to his office. "Sorry to be away so long," he apologized to Rance and Stacey. "I rode back to the ranch with Cassie. She's taken Farley's death pretty hard."

Both men gave assurances they understood. The sheriff then brought up a situation he hated. "Tomorrow is that crazy Barnum and Bailey nonsense in Snake Creek where I'm going to pose for pictures restaging the shoot out with Matt McCall. Bo Jefferson will also be there. Stacey, I'd like you to come along."

"My privilege, Sheriff. When I read the article in *The Saturday Evening Post*, I can reflect on how I was an eyewitness to it all."

Thad nodded his thanks, then looked at Dehner. "Rance, I'd like you to stay here in town. Much of Travis will be in Snake Creek tomorrow. Some jaspers may take advantage of that."

"Sounds like you're expecting serious trouble," Dehner remarked.

Jarrett threw his arms up in frustration. "You're damn right, I expect trouble. But I have no idea what kind of trouble. I can't pull the bones out of all this craziness."

The sheriff began to pace about the office. "The way things are going, I wouldn't be surprised if the ghost of Matt McCall did show up in Snake Creek tomorrow, dragging chains behind him like the ghost of Jacob Marley. Or maybe the son of Matt McCall will be sneaking around Travis, starting fires that will burn the town to ashes."

Jarrett hurled his hat against the back wall of the office, then sighed as it dropped to the floor. "I'm sorry, gents. It's just that I know something terrible is going to happen tomorrow. I don't know what, where or when. But I feel it deep down, something terrible is going to happen."

CHAPTER TWENTY

As Sheriff Thad Jarrett stood in the street of Snake Creek, exactly where he had stood twenty-two years before, he remembered the threat shouted at him by Music Matt McCall. "I'm paying a visit to my good friend, Satan. But I'll be back to even the score, Jarrett!" The lawman's hand hovered over his six gun, his mind thinking, "Come on back, McCall, nothing would make me happier than to kill you again."

"Not bad," Riley Bennett said aloud as he piloted a small buckboard on the way to Snake Creek. For the last few days, much of Riley's thoughts had been given over to composing an article about an event which had not yet taken place.

"I won't be riding bumpy dirt roads much longer," he proclaimed confidently to the two horses pulling the wagon. "Once the article appears, the *Post* will probably ask me to join their staff."

A sudden thought amended his previous musings. "I need to include a good word or two about Kain Arnell. He's the one who convinced the magazine to let me take the pictures and write the article."

Riley stopped speaking aloud as his thoughts

turned dark. There was something frightening about Kain Arnell. He remembered that night in the *Gazette* office when Kain had pressured him to prominently include a quote by Bradford Conrad in an article about the assault on the Bonners. Kain had smiled and his words were kind, but his eyes conveyed a quiet threat that still frightened Riley Bennett.

Riley's bad mood quickly dissipated as he rode into Snake Creek. He was hours early and only a few people had arrived before him, dotting what had become a ghost town. In the distance, he could spot the mayor of Travis talking to Bo Jefferson.

"Hello, Newspaper Man!"

"Hello, Doby." Riley pulled up the buckboard. Doby was a barfly who wasn't totally useless. He did various chores and odd jobs around town to pay for his liquor. As the bartender at the Dusty Trail put it, "Doby's a tramp, but he's not a freeloader."

Riley figured Doby had been given a job for the day and was not surprised when the barfly pointed toward the dilapidated building that had once been a livery. "I got that old place swept out good. Why dunt ya take your wagon in there? I'll tend to the horses."

"Thanks Doby," Riley said to the barfly as he turned the horses and rode the buckboard into the former livery. He rode past the empty stalls, then turned once again and parked the wagon sideways against the back wall.

Putting on the brake, Riley jumped off the buckboard and quickly walked around to the wagon's bed and the love of his life.

"What's that fancy lookin' object, Newspaper Man?"

"A Pearsall camera! It's the latest thing out of New York. Today, I'm going to use it to take pictures for *The Saturday Evening Post*!"

Riley paused, as if overwhelmed in wonderment by what was happening to him.

"Say, Newspaperman, who's gonna be the pretend Matt McCall?"

"Reade Bourke."

"How 'bout the shooter on the roof?"

"A ranch hand from—"

Red flashed across Riley's face. He collapsed to the ground, listening to an obscene chuckle from Doby. Then he felt his body being picked up and wondered where he was being taken. He lost consciousness before he got the answer.

Bo Jefferson and Stacey Hooper turned over a splintered wooden sign that was half buried in dust. Bo read the words on the sign aloud, " 'Red Dog Saloon.' Yes, this is where the gun fight took place." The pastor pointed across the street to where an overhang was, miraculously, still hanging. "That was Shad's Gun Shop, where I . . .

stood." Bo didn't want to say it was the location from which he had shot a gunman off the roof of the saloon.

Reade Bourke caressed his cheek thoughtfully as he looked behind him. "Guess I should walk from that direction."

The man's a genius, Thad Jarrett mused sarcastically about the man who could be his future son-in-law. He looked about for Cassie, but couldn't spot her. Not that he was surprised. Thad, along with Reade, Bo, and Stacey were setting up the staging in what had been the main street of Snake Creek. They were surrounded on both sides by mobs of people. The settlement had died before boardwalks were constructed, and horses were mingled with the crowd. Children were perched on the animals where they could have a good view.

Jarrett felt embarrassed and disgusted. His lawman's instincts were not quite clicking. Stacey Hooper was first to spot that something was amiss.

Hooper approached the two men who were setting up a camera on a tripod. "Good afternoon, gentlemen."

"Afternoon," one of them replied curtly.

Stacey quickly took in the photographers. They were both well dressed in recently purchased suits. Sunlight reflected off the new derbies that topped their heads. The new duds had obviously been purchased from the same store at the same time. They were dressed to look successful and important.

The countenances of the men did not match their attire. They were both in their early twenties with faces reflecting nervousness and even fear.

"Are you gentlemen working with Riley Bennett?" Stacey asked as Thad Jarrett joined him.

"No," the reply was once again curt and came from the same man who had spoken before.

His partner smiled and touched a finger to his derby. The interest being displayed by a legendary lawman changed everything. A more amicable approach was needed. "My name is Hadley; my colleague is Fred. We are from *The Saturday Evening Post*. The magazine decided to use their own staff rather than rely on an outsider."

Jarrett kept his voice in a neutral tone. "You've got one of those new Pearsall cameras, jus' like the one Riley Bennett uses."

Hadley gave his shoulders a broad shrug. "Not such a big coincidence, really. The Pearsall is taking over photography these days."

"Reckon so," Jarrett agreed. "Guess that's why Riley takes such good care of his camera. He's not quite so fussy about the tripod, though. He got a nick in one of the wooden legs." The sheriff pointed downward toward the tripod in front of him. "Why, it's jus' like the nick right there."

Hadley began to run. Thad tripped him. Hadley

hit the ground, then sprang to his feet and tried another dash. The sheriff grabbed him by the arm and threw a punch against the side of his head. Hadley went down again. This time he didn't spring up.

A Derringer popped into Stacey's hand. He pressed the short barrel of the gun against Fred's forehead.

Loud applause and cheers came from the surrounding crowd. "Ah, the voice of the people. They want more action and violence," Stacey informed his prisoner cheerfully. "You must not tempt me by trying an escape. I am a former actor, you know. I hate to disappoint an audience."

Thad jerked Hadley back onto his feet and marched him over to his companion and demanded, "What are you jaspers up to?"

The jaspers looked at each other as if wondering if it was too late to concoct a lie.

"I can at least partially answer your question, Sheriff," Stacey assured. "Notice the dark stains on the hands of both men. Stains that come from setting type and other tasks required of putting out a publication. They are journalists trying to steal a dream assignment away from another journalist." Stacey eyed the two prisoners. "Where do you gentlemen ply your trade?"

"Crow Branch," Hadley answered. "It's a two-hour ride west of here. Our paper failed. We couldn't get any advertising."

"We did get one advertiser," Fred corrected. "Sally the Sociable Seamstress ran a few ads. She was a whore. The law shut her down."

"Let me guess what happened then," Stacey broke in. "Having lost your advertising base, you closed your paper and came to Travis hoping to get jobs with the *Travis Gazette*."

"Yeh," Hadley continued the narrative. "Bennett didn't need help. But he showed off the Pearsall and told us all about his assignment from the *Post*."

"It didn't seem fair," Fred mumbled.

"Gentlemen, you should be ashamed of yourselves," Stacey declared with mock solemnity. "At this point in your lives you should be aware that life is not fair."

Thad Jarrett sighed with irritation. "On a less philosophical note, tell us what you've done with Riley Bennett."

Several of the attendees were in hearing range of the conversations between the lawmen and the failed journalists. A hot day, a large crowd and a festive atmosphere does not lend itself to the conveying of truth. As Thad pulled Doc Raikin out of the crowd and, accompanied by Stacey and Bo, began to follow Hadley and Fred, rumors circulated as to the gruesome death the two villains had inflicted on Riley Bennett.

Reality was less alarming. Riley was found bound and gagged, lying on the floor of what had once been the livery's office. When the gag was removed, his first words were, "The Pearsall, did they hurt the camera?!"

Doc Raikin patched Riley Bennett's head and diagnosed him capable of taking pictures for a national magazine. As he rose to his feet, Riley was contemplating how well events were favoring him. His story would not only be an account of what happened over twenty years ago. No! Now he could also write about an unprovoked attack on a member of the fourth estate. An attack that failed. He had bravely shaken off his injury and . . .

Bennett's mind was so engrossed in his story that he almost didn't notice the events taking place around him. As the group ambled out of the livery, Thad Jarrett spoke angrily to the two assailants.

"You say Doby took a fast ride after helping tie up Riley?"

Both unemployed newspapermen nodded their heads.

"That barfly better never show his face in Travis again," Thad declared.

The sheriff returned his anger to Hadley and Fred. "I think you fools are more stupid than dangerous. But you sure picked the wrong time to be stupid. There's too much crazy stuff going on right now to ignore something like this. Stacey, I want you to handcuff these jackasses, take them back to Travis and jail them. Bo and I can handle matters here."

"Aye, aye, Sheriff," Stacey proclaimed as he removed handcuffs from his belt. "While I have often been involved in the apprehension of evil doers, this is the first time I have been able to apply cuffs. I cherish the opportunity."

Hadley shouted at Thad, his voice ringing with pious indignation. "This is unlawful! You can't arrest a man for being stupid."

"Maybe not, but I'll make an exception in your case." Thad tossed Stacey another set of cuffs.

Thad, Bo, Riley, and the doctor returned to the crowd only to find that Kain Arnell had assumed center stage. Kain was jubilantly proclaiming the benefits the Conrad Western Railroad had bestowed upon the noble settlers of the west. Reade Bourke stood beside him, his face glowing contentment.

The crowd cheered Riley Bennett and his companions. Kain continued in a jubilant voice. "Mr. Bennett, we're so happy to see you safe. Sheriff Jarrett, be assured I have not used this occasion to make a political speech. No, I have only talked about the deep concern the Conrad Western Railroad has—"

"Yes, Mr. Arnell," Thad cut in. "I'm sure the widows and orphans of Arizona would have gone cold and hungry were it not for the benevolent actions of the Conrad Western Railroad!"

The crowd erupted in laughter. Kain Arnell looked angry. Reade Bourke looked uneasy.

Thad Jarrett looked pleased. "All that time spent listening to Stacey Hooper hasn't been completely wasted," he declared loudly.

Reade Bourke felt a sudden need to change the subject. "Let's get started!"

The mayor's shout sounded dramatic. But what followed was not. For all the hoopla the event had received, there was nothing very interesting about watching pictures being taken. Most folks began to saunter off and return home as Riley Bennett kept shouting at his subjects to hold still.

Stacey Hooper could tell something was wrong the moment he marched his prisoners into the sheriff's office. Rance Dehner's face was grim. Dehner remained grim as they locked Hadley and Fred up and then returned to the office.

Rance got to the point. "I got a reply from my telegram to the Lowrie Agency just before you returned." He picked up the paper from the desk and handed it to Stacey.

Hooper's turn to look grim. "Dear God. This changes everything."

Dehner sighed deeply. "It must have taken you at least an hour to get here. We'd need another hour to get back. That's too late. I just hope nothing really bad has happened."

"Yes, I hope so too . . ."

• • •

The sheriff accompanied Riley Bennett back to his buckboard. The lawman carried the tripod while Riley carefully toted his beloved Pearsall. Thad watched in amusement as the newspaperman gently wrapped the camera in blankets and set it on the flatbed of the wagon along with the tripod.

The lawman waved at Riley as he guided the buckboard out of the long-abandoned livery. The sheriff mused that Riley Bennett and his *Travis Gazette* had done a lot of good for the town. Jarrett knew that Bennett longed for a job with the *Post* and hoped he got it. Still, Thad admitted silently that he would miss the pesky but conscientious newspaperman.

Stepping out of the livery, Jarrett did a fast scan of the dwindling crowd now making their way to their wagons, buggies, and horses. He didn't spot Cassie. Of course, Reade Bourke wasn't around either. That shouldn't surprise him!

Thad smirked at his own irritation, then spoke to his desires, "Do you want grandkids or not?"

As he walked toward the dead tree where his horse was tied up, Thad wondered if the murder of Farley Canton would, somehow, hasten the marriage of his daughter to Bourke. He hadn't seen Cassie so emotional since her mother died.

Not until he was ready to mount did the lawman spot the envelope tied to the horn of his saddle.

The envelope lay on top of the saddle where it would not be spotted by casual passersby.

He hastily opened the envelope, pulled out the paper inside and read the contents. For the first time in decades, Thad Jarrett's hands shook. His breathing became ragged.

The sheriff inhaled deeply. Panic wouldn't help anyone. He had to calm himself. More than at any other time in his life, he had to do exactly the right thing.

CHAPTER TWENTY-ONE

Bo Jefferson didn't care much for Saturday nights. He'd look over his sermon notes for Sunday morning and always feel he should tear it all up and start over. And then there was his Sunday School superintendent, Ida Akers. Ida always made an appearance on Saturday night toting various items for the Sunday School lesson, which she insisted on setting up in advance.

Ida would use the opportunity to instruct the pastor on his many shortcomings. Bo particularly dreaded Ida's visit on this night. He knew what her subject would be. A man of God had no business taking part in some circus which glorified violence. Why, there had been children in Snake Creek this afternoon. What kind of a message was Travis' pastor giving them?

"Don't be so grouchy," the pastor reprimanded himself. "Ida and her husband do a lot of good for the church and the community."

Bo restlessly drummed his fingers on his home's one table. The notes in front of him might as well be written in Chinese. His mind journeyed to the many nights when Thad would ask for his help in keeping the lid on particularly rambunctious ranch hands. He didn't like to admit it to himself, but he did enjoy those crazy nights. The pastor wondered if stopping gunfights in saloons did more good than his sermons.

A pounding on the front door snapped him back to the present. The knocks were too loud for Ida Akers.

Jefferson was shocked when he opened the door. The man standing in front of him was pale and quivering, with desperate eyes. "Thad, you look awful..."

"Good." The sheriff stormed into the room. "I jus' told Dehner and Hooper that I'm sick and going to the ranch to rest. They've got to believe me."

"Why? I don't—"

"Read this—" Jarrett pulled a sheet of paper out of a large envelope and placed it on the table.

"Oh, dear God," Jefferson whispered as he read the note, neatly written in ink.

> WE HAVE CASSIE. IF YOU WANT HER BACK ALIVE BE AT LIGHTNING ROCK AT MIDNIGHT. BRING THE PREACHER. NO ONE ELSE. COME UNARMED. WE HAVE ALREADY KILLED. NOTHING TO LOSE.

Bo struggled to cope with the horror in front of him. "I don't recognize the handwriting, do you?"

"Of course I don't recognize it! We're dealing with a gang. Whoever is running the show dictated that note, letter by letter, to some stupid thug. I've read that thing a million times by now. Not one word is misspelled."

Jarrett threw his arms up and began pacing the room. "Damn! Everything those outlaws who attacked you said, is coming true. They started with someone I only cared about for what I could learn from him and now they've got Cassie."

The lawman stopped and rubbed his forehead. "Everything's crazy. We have a ransom note not mentioning money. And they demand you come along!"

Jefferson spoke softly. "Maybe it's not crazy."

"What do you mean?"

"You don't think about it much, Thad, but you're a wealthy man. You own one half of the Circle J."

Intelligence flamed in Jarrett's eyes, replacing the panic. "Yes. Cassie owns the other half."

Bo continued, "Maybe whoever is behind this wants you and Cassie to sign a document of some kind turning the Circle J over to him. Having a pastor's name on the document as a witness would help if someone challenged its authenticity."

Thad made a fist with his right hand and slammed it into his left palm. "You've only got a theory, but it's a good one. Doesn't explain everything, but it makes sense. You can bet the snake behind all this already has a plan for Cassie and me to die tonight. He'll also have to kill you."

"We'll cross that bridge when we come to it. Don't worry about me. After all, tomorrow is Sunday. Nothing can stand between a preacher and his weekly chance to pound the pulpit."

The bravado helped stabilize Thad Jarrett. He nodded a thank you and fell silent for a few moments before speaking. "Lightning Rock is about a thirty-minute ride from here. We've four hours or so before midnight. We'll leave now and hide out in that area and see what we can spot. Never mind that stuff about being unarmed."

Bo hastily made his way to a cabinet. "I'll get my guns."

As his friend was strapping on his gun belt, Thad Jarrett glanced at the sermon notes on the table. "I sure hope you get to pound that pulpit tomorrow morning."

CHAPTER TWENTY-TWO

Lightning Rock fronted a large cluster of boulders at the side of a narrow trail. The trail was dotted with several patches of rocks separated by swathes of hard land as if the stones had formed hostile tribes.

Lightning Rock towered over its companions. At the top of its almost twelve feet was a series of small cracks covered by blackness. An old story claimed the boulder had once been struck by lightning. Like many old stories, it was now accepted as truth.

Thad and Bo tied up their horses in a clump of trees, then walked almost a quarter mile to a nest of boulders directly across from Lightning Rock. Both men then positioned themselves behind one of the large stones and waited for something to happen. Thad checked his pocket watch.

"Eight-fifteen. Patience is a big part of being a lawman," he whispered. Those were the last words either man spoke for over three and a half hours.

They were watching a trail that saw little use. They had been there less than an hour when Jug, a local moonshiner, piloted his small wagon past them. Jug had gone into Travis for his usual Saturday sales and was now returning to his remote still.

A bright moon made it possible for both men to occasionally check their watches and monitor the frustratingly slow trudge of time. Moments after Bo had noted it was ten minutes after eleven, hoofbeats could be heard coming from the direction of town.

A lone rider approached. A red ember hurled sparks into the wind. The rider was enjoying a smoke.

The smoker pulled up in front of Lightning Rock. He leaned back as if in an easy chair and inhaled on what, even from a distance, could now be seen as a cigarillo. He held the cigarillo in front of him approvingly, then returned it to his mouth.

The rider suddenly seemed to become aware of time. He hastily pulled an envelope from one of his saddle bags, dismounted and hurried behind the rock.

Thad and Bo exchanged quick glances. Guns in hands, they quietly made their way across the trail. Each man took one side of Lightning Rock and made his way around it.

"Hands up!" Jarrett shouted at a man whose face was partially covered with smoke.

"Whatever you say, Sheriff," Kain Arnell replied in what to Jefferson sounded like a disturbingly cheerful voice.

The pastor moved quickly to where he, like Thad, was facing Kain Arnell. The experience wasn't pleasant. Arnell beamed a cruel, hard, smile. Not the look you'd expect from a cornered outlaw.

Jarrett pointed at the envelope in Arnell's right hand. "I suppose that envelope contains instructions on where to go next. You were going to have us ride around for an hour or so before we got to where you've hidden Cassie."

Arnell's cigarillo tipped back and forth at the corner of his mouth as he spoke. "You suppose wrong, Sheriff. Completely wrong."

"Then what's in it?" Thad demanded.

"If you'll allow me to lower my hand, Sheriff Jarrett, I will give the envelope to Reverend Jefferson. He can read the contents out loud."

"Go ahead, damn you!"

Keeping his gun pointed at Kain Arnell, Bo took the envelope and yanked out a sheet of paper, allowing the envelope to drop to the ground. The writing on the paper was large. It was intended to be read by moonlight.

Bo closed his eyes for a second, then read, "Drop your guns. You're surrounded."

Three men appeared from the boulders behind Thad and Bo. They laughed as they walked toward their prisoners.

Kain Arnell joined in the merriment. He dropped his hands downward while sharing a laugh with the three thugs now standing behind the lawman and the pastor.

He once again inhaled leisurely on the cigarillo. "I would follow those instructions, gents. After all, there are three killers inches behind you. If you move your trigger fingers at all they will fill the backs of your heads with hot lead. That would leave Cassie Jarrett completely at our mercy. Drop the guns now!"

"I'm sorry, Bo," the sheriff said as both men followed instructions. "I should have anticipated this."

"The night isn't over yet, Thad," Jefferson's voice rang with a confidence he didn't really have.

Jarrett looked at his captor. "You must think you're very smart."

"Not really," Arnell replied. "I just work for a smart boss. All this is my boss' idea, including the drop your guns note. Nice touch, don't you think?"

"You stink like a pile of pig manure, Arnell," Jarrett shouted. "I'm warning you, if Cassie has even been scratched—"

Kain Arnell stepped toward the lawman. He pressed the tip of his cigarillo between Jarrett's eyes. "Keep your damn mouth shut, Mr. Living Legend. From now on, I call the shots and you obey the master."

Arnell tossed the smoke to the ground. "You understand, Mr. Living Legend?"

Hatred for his enemy deadened the burning

pain on the lawman's forehead. "I understand."

The Conrad Western Railroad's hired killer was enjoying himself. "Make that, 'I understand, Sir.' "

Jarrett didn't hesitate. Resistance couldn't come until he located Cassie and knew her situation. "I understand, Sir."

"Did you hear that, men?!" Arnell shouted to the three gunmen working with him. "You can tell your grandkids you rode with the jasper who brought down the great Thad Jarrett!"

The gun slicks didn't look all that impressed. Irritation became evident in the killer's voice as he spoke directly to his prisoners. "We're gonna get our horses, then you two are going to show us where your nags are tied up. After that, we'll blindfold you and take a little ride."

The ride was a dark nightmare for Thad Jarrett. A small trickle of blood oozed down the bridge of his nose from the burn Arnell's cigarillo had inflicted on the space between his eyes.

Only a little blood was being lost. Thad's anguish had a different source. Two people he cared about deeply could lose their lives tonight. And all because of him. His lawman's instincts had failed when Cassie was kidnapped. He had handled the situation poorly.

Those instincts were now back and only bringing bad news. Thad Jarrett had long ago developed an understanding of outlaws. Some were desperate men, breaking the law to survive. Some were confused kids who could be reformed.

But Kain Arnell and his thugs didn't belong in those categories. They were savages who had long ago lost any sense of decency. They relished killing. And now his daughter and his best friend were captives of these men. *I've got to keep calm, come up with a way out of this,* the sheriff thought to himself. *A jittery lawman is no good to anyone.*

"We'll tie up here!" Those were the first words Kain Arnell had spoken since the ride began. Jarrett noted that the killer felt no need to whisper.

Thad was yanked off his saddle but still managed to land on his feet. It did him no good. Something hard crashed against one of his ankles and he dropped to the ground.

"My, my, Living Legend, you seem to be having trouble staying upright tonight." Jarrett recognized the voice of Kain Arnell as he got back onto his feet.

Kain continued, "Now, there are still guns pointed at you and your friend so don't get any crazy notions while we take those blindfolds off.

Jarrett blinked off dust from the bandanna that had served as a blindfold and looked around. He first sighted a grove of skeletal trees he had once jokingly called "the ugliest trees in Arizona." Horses were now tied to those ugly trees.

"We're on the Circle J!"

"That's right, Living Legend, I know the Circle J is a big ranch and you spend most of your days in town, but you really should take a close look at your land more often." Using his gun as a pointer, Arnell motioned to his right. "We're going to do a little inspection right now."

Thad and Bo walked together, surrounded by three gunmen and Arnell. They made their way along a wooden fence, which separated the ranch from farmland used by homesteaders. Thad and Bo viewed the farmland carefully, then exchanged chagrined looks. The nearest farmhouse was a long way off. Not much chance of farmers coming to their aid.

They approached two recently built line shacks. Thad once again experienced surprise. To call the structures standing about twelve feet apart, "shacks," was doing them an injustice. They were unusually large and well-built for line shacks.

Through the nearest side window, Jarrett saw a yellow light flickering. Shadows moved inside. They were expected.

Arnell now walked ahead of the procession. He tapped with his gun on the door and received a shout from inside, "Come in."

As they stepped inside, Jarrett assessed the situation as best he could. There was a curtainless window on each side of the cabin, allowing for a breeze. But on this night, both windows were closed. On a shelf over one window perched a lantern, which provided a patch of light augmented by a bright moon.

Kain ordered Bo and Thad to stand close together. The three gunmen remained silent and behind them.

Kain was not silent. He stepped toward a man who stood near the back of the shack on the periphery of the light, and stood beside him, proclaiming in a mocking voice, "The guests of honor have arrived, Mr. Mayor!"

"Reade Bourke," Jarrett's voice was hard and contemptuous. "I should have known it was you behind all this."

"There's a lotta things you shoulda' knowed, Sheriff." Bourke turned his head to look behind him.

A figure disconnected from the back wall of the shack. Thad and Bo could make out little more than an outline as the apparition moved toward them.

The figure halted in the light from the lantern, like a performer centered in the spotlight. Now the two captives could see who they were facing. The apparition was clothed entirely in black, including a hood and gloves. One of those gloved hands held a pistol.

Jefferson looked closely at the eyes and mouth visible through the hood. But the glare of the lantern cast a grotesque yellow over those small portions of the face. He couldn't even guess the identity of the gunney.

There quickly turned out to be no reason to guess. The gunney's free hand gradually pulled off the hood.

"Dear God," Bo whispered.

Thad Jarrett could only manage a painful groan which came from deep inside as if a sharp blade had cut his soul.

A screeching maniacal laugh filled the shack. "Meet the cold-blooded killer behind all the murders plaguing Travis, Arizona, Lawman," shouted Cassie Jarrett.

CHAPTER TWENTY-THREE

"Father, now I can torture and kill you, and not feel a touch of guilt," Cassie's voice remained a shout. Her face twisted in hatred.

Both Thad Jarrett and Bo Jefferson stood pale and stunned, unable to recognize the demonic creature who paced about in front of them.

Cassie moved a step closer to her father, but remained a safe distance away. The woman appeared insane but still aware that she faced a veteran lawman.

"Mother really did love you, Father. In the way a little girl loves a stray puppy."

She stepped back, lifted her gun hand up and waved the weapon in a circle. Neither captive responded to the move. That seemed to anger the woman.

"Yes Father, while you were in town earning peanuts like a monkey in the circus, your wife built a prosperous ranch. And she taught me everything she had to learn for herself. What did you ever teach me? How to obey the law?"

The woman began to pace back and forth in front of the two captives. "But in one way, you were a big help to me and Mother. Do you know how?"

"No. Why don't you tell me, Cassie?"

"You kept us amused, Lawman! Remember three years ago when the town council raised your pay from forty to sixty dollars a month? You were so grateful to the people of Travis for showing such confidence in you. That was a big day in your life!"

The woman tried to laugh. It came out a screech. "Mother and I had to work at not laughing in your face. Sixty dollars a month, pathetic!"

"You must have a powerful hate for me, Daughter."

"Yes Father, I do. But Mother loved you and for her sake, I didn't want to kill you. I begged you to take that job in St. Louis. The pay was respectable, and you wouldn't have to sleep on a cot in a miserable office four nights a week."

As the young woman raged, Bo Jefferson tried to dispel his shock and find a way out. He couldn't do either. He did notice that Reade Bourke, Kain Arnell, and the trio of armed thugs standing behind him and Thad didn't seem surprised by Cassie's tirade. They were accustomed to her madness.

Jefferson decided to stall for time, even though he had no idea what to do with the time. "There's another reason you wanted your father to leave for St. Louis, isn't there, Cassie? You wanted him far away, so you could fix the referendum, and bring in the railroad."

"That's how it started, Preacher Man," Cassie

stopped and turned her gun toward Bo. "Then Kain Arnell arrived in town. We quickly became, shall we say, business associates. Mr. Arnell knows how to buy votes. I'm not worried one bit about the referendum."

"Then why were you so anxious to get rid of me?" Thad Jarrett's voice resounded with heavy despair.

Cassie's eyes flashed anger. "Because, Father dear, Mother loved you and that put a lid on her ambition. I don't love you, never have."

The woman looked at Reade and Kain as if they needed to pay special attention to her words. "I'm not satisfied with being a successful rancher. I want to own this territory. Reade and I will combine our ranches and destroy anyone who opposes us. We may employ Mr. Arnell's services. First matter of business: get rid of the homesteaders."

Thad's response was reflexive. "You can't do that!"

This time, Cassie's laughter sounded joyous. "Oh yes we can! You're going to die tonight, Sheriff Jarrett. Reade Bourke, the honorable mayor of Travis, will take charge of appointing your successor and his deputy."

Cassie looked briefly at Bo Jefferson, then returned her eyes to Thad. "Remember how you first got the job of sheriff? You and the preacher had to throw out two crooked lawmen. Soon, two crooked lawmen will be taking your place. Your whole life has been wasted, Father!"

The woman's face contorted. For a moment, she appeared to be stifling a cry. But when she spoke her voice remained mockingly cheerful.

"Of course, the good citizens of Travis will demand to know how their legendary lawman and beloved sky pilot died. Would you like to hear the story we will give them?"

Neither captive responded. Cassie began to pace once again. "People will be told that Thad Jarrett, while showing off his fast draw, accidentally killed Bo Jefferson. The sheriff could not live with the disgrace of it all, so he took his own life."

"You wouldn't do that, Cassie . . ."

"Oh yes I will, Preacher Man." Cassie looked toward Arnell. They did a quick exchange of guns. Cassie was now holding her father's Colt .44. "I've already thought about how I'm going to tell the story to Riley Bennett. There will be tears in my eyes. Yes, I think the shameful death of a once legendary lawman will be on the front page of newspapers throughout the country."

Jefferson suddenly became overwhelmed by anger for his friend. Thad Jarrett was a man of great honor and his daughter wanted to turn him into a figure of mockery.

Bo stepped toward the woman. "Cassie, I've known you since birth. I held you when you were a baby. You don't really—"

Cassie slammed the Colt hard into Bo's face. The pastor staggered sideways and dropped to the floor. Thad started to move but his daughter cocked the gun. It made a harsh clicking sound. She pointed the Colt directly at her father.

"Stay right there," she ordered. "Remember what I told you, Father. I'm not only going to kill you, I'm going to torture you. Know how I plan to do it?"

"I've got my suspicions."

"You have a crazy need to protect people, Father. Too bad. Your final moments on earth will be spent watching your best friend take a bullet in the chest. It's your fault, and there's nothing you can do about it."

Bo Jefferson lay injured on the floor. Cassie, gun in hand, walked toward Jefferson and paused as she stood directly over him, positioning herself in order to watch her father's reaction when she fired.

Thad Jarrett's eyes darted about frantically as they took in every corner of the shack. He spotted Rance Dehner in the side window behind him. Dehner nodded, then ducked out of sight. The sheriff surmised that Stacey Hooper was at the other window, behind Cassie, but couldn't be sure.

Thad moved to the center of the light where his daughter had been only moments before. "Don't reckon I'll stay much longer, Cassie."

"What do you mean?"

While still facing his daughter, Thad began to step backwards toward the window where he had spotted Dehner. "Think I'll crash outta the window behind me." He spoke in a loud voice as he continued to move backwards. "The way I see it, cuts from glass are preferable to a bullet."

Cassie stepped away from Jefferson and returned to the yellow light which was now flickering. She walked toward her father as she pointed his .44 at him. Sensing that the woman was only seconds from killing her father, Reade Bourke, Kain Arnell, and the three gunneys did fast shuffles away from the lawman. Thad Jarrett now stood alone between his daughter and the side window.

Cassie moved close to her father as she lifted the .44. "I think a bullet in the head . . ."

Thad Jarrett cried uncontrollably as he plunged to the floor. Crashing glass and gunfire created a massive explosion in the shack. Red flashes cut the darkness. Cassie Jarrett stumbled backwards. Touching her stomach, she then raised her hand and stared at the blood-stained palm.

She looked at her father still lying on the floor. Her face was now knifed with pain. But hatred still poured from her eyes. "You damn . . ." She folded and collapsed.

While Dehner had fired at Cassie, Stacey Hooper had placed a bullet in a thug standing near Jefferson. When the outlaw fell, Jefferson did a fast roll toward him and grabbed the pistol now lying beside the fallen thug's hand. He fired at one of the crooks who was now firing at Hooper. Another hired killer hit the floor.

Reade Bourke crouched in darkness at the back of the cabin, "Kill them, kill them all!"

Only one thug remained to follow orders and he wasn't about to die for a lost cause. The gunman dropped his weapon and raised his hands.

Dehner remained outside and watched as Stacey Hooper slithered through the window opposite him and took charge. Smoke and the smell of cordite drifted through the window and enveloped the detective. Hooper helped Bo to his feet, then handcuffed the one standing outlaw.

But Rance's attention was fixed on Thad Jarrett. The sheriff was now on his knees beside his daughter's corpse. One hand gently caressed her face. "Cassie . . . Cassie . . ."

Behind him, Dehner could hear neighing horses. He glanced backwards and saw Kain Arnell untying one of the horses at the grove of trees.

Inside the shack, Reade Bourke was starting to blather nonsense about being forced to act against his will. Dehner shouted to be heard over him. "Keep things in line here, Stacey. I'll be back!"

Hooper's reply was immediate. "Yes, I've noticed that one of our participants departed prematurely. Do all you can to hasten his return."

Dehner ran to the trees and freed his bay. As he mounted, he could hear hoofbeats receding into the darkness. He kneed the horse into a fast run.

CHAPTER TWENTY-FOUR

Kain Arnell backed his horse up, then jumped the fence. He felt safer riding through farmland. Farmers sleep at night. Ranch hands are up and about as they take different watches over the cattle.

His roan was strong and hadn't been ridden hard that day. He stood a good chance of getting away.

Arnell spurred the horse viciously. The animal's hooves destroyed crops barely sprouting up from the flat ground.

Kain did a fast glance backwards. His hopes of a pursuer not noticing the abrupt turn were squelched. He was being chased, probably by Dehner, whose face he had spotted briefly as shots provided flames of light in the shack.

Panic enveloped the killer who was in unfamiliar danger. In the past, his fine dress and wholesome good looks had always allowed him to leave the scene unnoticed after secretly committing murder. There had been no need for escape.

Arnell took another backward glance. The enemy was gaining on him, and yes, he was pretty sure it was Dehner.

Kain Arnell suddenly realized he was playing

the detective's game. Dehner probably had plenty of experience chasing an adversary on horseback.

So, why not change the rules?

Arnell recalled his circus days. Instead of trying to ride from Dehner, he would ride directly at the detective. As he drew near, he'd slip off the saddle and hang onto the horn with one hand. The horse would be his shield.

Kain Arnell felt confident that he understood Dehner. The detective was the type who would hesitate to shoot a horse, even though the horse shielded a man who was trying to kill him. The hesitation might be for only a moment.

But a moment would be all he needed.

Kain pulled up his roan. He gave the animal a quick pat as he assessed the situation. Dehner was still riding toward him at a fast speed.

Arnell turned his roan and rode directly at his enemy. If Dehner was surprised by the move, he showed no sign of it. He kept his bay at a gallop, quickly reducing the amount of ground between him and Kain Arnell.

Timing was everything. The moment he was in firing range of Dehner, Arnell lifted a gun from his holster, slid off his saddle, clamped his legs together and prepared to take a shot at the detective.

A shot fired while Arnell was adjusting the gun in his hand. The roan went up on hind legs. The gun flew out of Arnell's hand as his body twirled into the air then smashed onto the ground. The roan's front legs came down and it ran off.

Rance Dehner palmed his gun as he watched Arnell charge at him. Despite the circumstances, Dehner was momentarily impressed by Arnell's skills at trick riding as he watched the killer vanish onto one side of his horse. Still, Dehner needed to bring the act to a fast climax.

The detective fired a bullet which burrowed into the ground in front of Arnell's roan. The animal reared up and spun the trickster off his saddle. As the horse galloped off, Dehner saw Arnell splayed ignominiously over the ground. His gun lay a few yards away from him.

The killer was dazed but very aware of his predicament. He scrambled to his feet and, weaving only slightly, ran toward the gun.

Rance still had his Colt .45 in hand. But he had witnessed enough gunfire for one night. He rode toward the killer, leaped from his bay, and collided with Arnell while the killer was still a yard away from his weapon.

Dehner was first onto his feet. He slammed his Colt against the back of Arnell's head. The killer remained conscious but was no longer a threat. Rance retrieved the killer's gun, then spoke in an almost admiring tone.

"That was quite an impressive stunt you pulled.

Were you ever a trick rider?"

Kain was slowly sitting up. "Yeh, I used to be in a circus."

"The dream of every boy," Dehner replied. "To run off and join the circus."

The detective sighed wistfully. "I reckon it was a tough life. Still, you should have stayed with the dream."

Arnell's roan hadn't run off very far. Getting the killer back to the shacks on the Circle J wasn't difficult. Reade Bourke watched them approach with a grim expression. Bourke's hands had been tied behind his back. Reade's story about being forced to participate in the scheme to kill Thad Jarrett was believed by no one. And the testimony of Kain Arnell wasn't going to help. The mayor had been hoping Arnell would escape or be killed. Either option had been fine with him.

Dehner and his prisoner pulled up as the sheriff approached them. "I'll take this owlhoot off your hands, Rance."

Jarrett's voice was calm but eerily superficial. Dehner nodded his head as the sheriff helped Arnell dismount. The killer was woozy from the head wound Dehner had inflicted on him.

Rance slid off his horse and tied it up in the grove of trees along with Kain's roan. He then surveyed the scene.

No one was talking. The outlaw who had

surrendered was lying, handcuffed, in front of the first shack where the shooting had taken place. Stacey was tying the outlaw's feet. Apparently, the crook had tried to run off. Thad Jarrett was leading Kain toward Stacey. Dehner smiled slightly. His friend was about to go from being a jailer to dispensing medical care.

Mayor Bourke was leaning against the front corner of the shack as if trying to distance himself from the grubby goings on all around him. His face was gray with defeat.

Bo Jefferson was attending to the bed of a buckboard he must have retrieved from the ranch's barn. Dehner approached the wagon.

Bo had just placed a large canvas over the bed. The pastor sensed Rance's question before he asked it. "Two of the gunmen are dead. And . . ." Bo stopped speaking and gestured toward a much smaller bulge in the canvas.

Dehner stepped to the side of the wagon and lifted the cover. It was something the detective had to do. He pressed his lips together as he looked down at the face of Cassie Jarrett. After a moment, he gently let the canvas back down.

"Cassie is the first woman I have ever killed," Dehner whispered. "Pray to God, she will be the last."

"I'll do just that," Reverend Jefferson replied.

Dehner took a brief look at the moon. It appeared to be moving, as if wanting to escape the grimness below.

Rance continued to speak in a whisper as he looked back at the pastor. "Do you think Cassie was honest about her mother's feelings? Could Linda Jarrett have been that contemptuous of her husband?"

"I don't know," Bo whispered back. "From time-to-time Linda complimented her husband on keeping the peace, which made ranching and all business easier. But that could have been an act, like it obviously was with Cassie. I got along with Linda just fine, but I never really thought I knew her. She was always sort of distant. One thing is for certain, Thad will go through the rest of his life wondering if Cassie told the truth about Linda. How that girl must have hated her father."

"She hated him all right."

"What do you mean?"

Dehner paused, ran his hand along the side of the buckboard, then spoke. "It all happened in a few seconds. I had to shoot Cassie twice. When she took the first bullet, she realized Thad had tricked her. With what little strength she had left, she tried to shoot her father. A second bullet was needed to stop that. The final moments of her life were devoted to trying to kill Thad Jarrett."

CHAPTER TWENTY-FIVE

Cassie Jarrett was buried at sunup the next day. Besides the gravediggers, Bo Jefferson and Thad Jarrett were the only ones present. That's the way Thad wanted it.

Rumors exploded across Travis and the Sunday morning service at Travis Community Church started late. People were mingling outside of the church, gossiping.

Bo Jefferson stifled his anger at the congregation. After all, the events of the previous night were shocking. Folks naturally wanted to know exactly what had happened. The pastor admitted to himself that some events in the nightmare had him confused. Like everyone else, he felt a compulsion to know the facts.

Bo sat on the church's platform and looked at the restless collection of souls finally settling into the pews. Before standing up to begin the service, he whispered to himself, "We'll know all the terrible news soon enough."

The pastor's sermon, a spontaneous affair, was on knowing the truth and how, in the deepest sense, the truth sets you free. "Even when the truth is something you'd rather not hear."

He ended his message in a cryptic manner. "Sheriff Jarrett is not with us today and he will not be on duty again until Tuesday. Deputies Rance Dehner and Stacey Hooper will be filling in and I will provide them with assistance if need be. Meanwhile, I encourage all of you to read the Monday edition of the *Travis Gazette*. The newspaper will provide all known facts about the tragedies which have ravaged our community. Our closing hymn is . . ."

Riley Bennett, Bo Jefferson, and Stacey Hooper stood in the sheriff's office sipping coffee and shifting their weight from one foot to the other. All conversation had been exhausted. The three men looked anxiously at Rance Dehner as he entered the office.

"Did you see Thad Jarrett?" Bennett blurted out.

"No."

Jefferson's voice was calmer. "Is the town settling down?"

"Pretty much," Dehner walked over to the stove and poured himself a cup of java. "A few people tried to pry information from me. But most of Travis' good citizens have had their lunch and gone home. They're content to wait for tomorrow's paper. I had a routine round."

The pastor pulled out his pocket watch. "Seven minutes before three-thirty. Thad is punctual . . . when he can be. Still, the man has been through a lot . . ."

Bo's excuse for his friend was unnecessary. Thad Jarrett walked into the office a minute or so before the agreed meeting time.

The sheriff's face was pale and void of emotion. Since he had wept over Cassie's dead body the night before, Thad Jarrett had kept a lock on showing any grief. At his daughter's burial that morning, the lawman's face had contorted briefly as the coffin was lowered into the ground. But the expression vanished as Thad waved to his longtime friend and walked away in haste.

Bo understood that something vital had been ripped from Thad Jarrett's soul. He could only pray that someday it would return.

Out of habit, the sheriff walked behind his desk. He remained standing as he spoke in a soft but firm voice. "Gentlemen, we have an important task in front of us. On Tuesday, the citizens of this town will vote on a referendum that will decide the future of Travis for years to come."

Jarrett looked downwards for a moment, then continued. "There has been a lot of brutality and death over the railroad controversy. People need to know the facts about all the bloodshed this town has suffered before they vote. I can't provide all those facts myself. But I'm sure the four of us, sharing what we know, can."

Thad turned to face the newspaperman who had removed a notebook from his coat pocket. "Riley, as we discussed earlier, I want you to print everything of value that you hear in this meeting. Don't be gentle. Maybe it's time people learn that a living legend gets saddle sores like everyone else!"

Jarrett pressed his lips together, then glanced quickly across the office. "That goes for all of you. There are a lot more important matters here than my feelings." He pointed at the detective. "Rance, you seem to have most pieces of the puzzle."

Dehner nodded his head. "Cassie Jarrett wanted to be the queen of a cattle empire, to be a law unto herself."

"The day of the cattle barons who rule like a king, or queen, are pretty much over," Jefferson commented. "What with the homesteading laws..."

"Cassie didn't see it that way," Dehner cut in. "But having a railroad run through Travis was a necessary part of her dream. She teamed up with Reade Bourke and they schemed to win the election... no matter how the voting went."

Riley Bennett pointed his pencil in Rance's direction. "But that would be impossible with Thad Jarrett as sheriff."

"Exactly," Dehner agreed. "And Cassie knew how to get rid of her father. Thad Jarrett had to believe that by staying in Travis he would put the lives of people he cared about in danger. But she couldn't carry it out."

The newspaperman's face crunched in confusion. "I don't follow you."

"Cassie didn't know how to contact the necessary gang to pull it off," Dehner explained. "So she hired Vern Tobin, a saddle bum. All that changed when Kain Arnell arrived. Somehow, Arnell and Cassie connected. They understood each other. Arnell had no trouble hiring a gang of five professional killers, though it took him a while to get them here. Vern Tobin became the first victim of the new scheme."

Bo Jefferson looked doubtful. "But by then, it would be too late. Even if Thad did quit, he wouldn't leave before the referendum."

"Arnell changed the plans," Dehner continued. "He was confident he could buy the election. But Cassie's dream of an empire couldn't be realized with her father around."

Riley Bennett understood. "And Kain Arnell wanted to be part of that empire."

Dehner nodded. "Reade Bourke remained a player, but a minor one. He took orders. Once Arnell got his helpers in place, Cassie's idea began to take hold: it started with the assault on Bo, and the phony story about Matt McCall's son living in Travis."

Rance shrugged his shoulders, then continued. "In a way, luck was on their side. The kidnapping of Tracey Bonner failed, but one of the hired thugs involved got away while the other one was killed."

"That was luck," Jefferson agreed. "Neither crook was captured, so no one blabbed to the law."

"The murder of Farley Canton was more complicated," Dehner said. "It was a last desperate attempt to get the sheriff to leave town. The hope was that Thad would be horrified by Farley's violent death and vow to leave town after the referendum, knowing Cassie would probably be the next target."

Rance paused; Thad Jarrett spoke to him in an encouraging voice. "Go ahead Rance, we are here to find out the whole truth."

"The gang members killed Farley. But Cassie arranged for you, Thad, to be at the ranch on the morning Farley's body was dumped there."

Jarrett gave a brittle laugh of total despair. "Afraid I messed up their plan. I was up early instead of being in bed when the savages arrived with poor Farley's corpse."

For a moment the sheriff moved his hands across the battered desktop in front of him, as if playing a musical instrument. His eyes seemed to be looking inward. "I surprised the gang. Shot one of them. I could have had a good shot at another one, but my daughter started screaming. I forgot the thugs and ran to her. She was a good deceiver . . ."

The lawman's voice trailed off and there was an awkward silence in the office. Riley Bennett shattered it. "Where did all this hullabaloo about *The Saturday Evening Post* fit in?"

"The whole set up with the *Post* was phony," Dehner answered. "If the sheriff had agreed to leave town, it would just have become a meaningless charade. But Thad didn't agree and the whole affair became the opening move in murdering the town's sheriff."

Bo Jefferson sighed deeply. "I can see that. The festive affair threw Thad off balance. Without all the nonsense, Thad would have been more cautious and thoughtful."

Riley Bennett's face went totally pale, mourning the loss of a dream. "You mean, all that talk about the *Post* was a lie?"

"Afraid so," Rance shot back. "I was fooled in the beginning, but my . . . associate . . . immediately became suspicious."

Dehner waved a hand in the direction of Stacey Hooper, whose face, as usual, sported a look of smug amusement. Curiously, Stacey's demeanor was not offensive but cast a welcome tinge of levity over a grim proceeding.

"In my reckless youth, I was a member of the acting profession," Stacey confessed. "Many of my fellow performers dreamed of having an article about them appear in the *Saturday Evening Post*. It would be a gateway to certain fame."

Riley looked confused. "Okay, but . . ."

"I immediately became suspicious of Kain

Arnell's claim that because the Conrad Western Railroad advertised in the *Post*, he had vast influence over the magazine. Yes, every publication needs advertisers to survive and flourish. But a prominent magazine like *The Saturday Evening Post* would hardly need to jump at the suggestion of one advertiser. I encouraged Rance to wire his employer, the Lowry Detective Agency, to investigate the matter."

"I received the reply on the day of the festival," Rance added. "The *Post* had no plans for an article about the shootout in Snake Creek. They had never heard of Kain Arnell."

Thad looked at his hands for a moment, then shifted his eyes to the gambler. "Great work, Stacey. I'm sure glad Rance brought you along."

The lawman had pulled himself out of grief for a moment to thank a man he didn't understand. Most gamblers were trouble, but not Stacey Hooper.

Grimness returned to Thad's face as he spoke to both of his volunteer deputies. "I thought I did a good job of convincing you gents that I was sick Saturday night. How'd you know I was in trouble?"

Dehner gave the sheriff a kind smile. "You and Bo owe your lives to a lady named Ida Akers. Apparently, Mrs. Akers visits the pastor's house every Saturday night to set up for her Sunday school class."

Stacey picked up the narrative. "But last Saturday the pastor wasn't home. Ida left, then returned twenty minutes later in the event Bo Jefferson had been attending to what the dear lady primly called, 'private matters.' Her persistence was in vain."

"Ida did a fast walk to the sheriff's office and convinced us Bo was in trouble," Rance said. "And Thad, you hadn't been all that convincing with your claims of being sick. You said you were going back to the Circle J to rest. Not knowing what else to do, Stacey and I went to the ranch. We ended up talking to your cook, who told us you weren't there."

Rance Dehner paused once again. The detective hated what had to come next. "Some things Cassie said had stayed with me . . ."

Thad tried to help, "Sort of like a pebble in the boot?"

"Yes," Rance continued. "On our first visit to the Circle J, Cassie told us she had been building line shacks along the border with the homesteaders."

"I remember," the sheriff acknowledged.

"Then, a few days ago, Cassie mentioned to Stacey and me that the land near the homesteaders was no longer fit for cattle grazing. So, why build line shacks in that area? I suppose there could have . . ."

Sensing Rance's discomfort, Stacey cut in.

"As we talked with the cook, it dawned on my detective friend that those line shacks could provide a hideout for the gang brought in to run Thad Jarrett out of town. The cook told us where the border was between Circle J and the homesteaders. Upon arrival, we quickly realized there were deadly goings on inside one of those shacks."

Thad Jarrett clenched both of his hands into fists, then stared at them as if wondering what purpose they served. "You can finish this meeting without me." He looked directly at Riley Bennett. "These gentlemen can tell you exactly what happened at the line shack last night. Print all of it."

Jarrett hastily left the office. Bo Jefferson took a few steps toward following him, then stopped, realizing his friend's need for solitude. An almost reverent silence fell over the room as the four men listened to Jarrett's departing footsteps.

The voice of a child suddenly cut the air. "Howdy, Sheriff Jarrett."

The footsteps stopped. "Hello, Tommy."

"You weren't in church, today."

"No, but I'll be there next Sunday. How are your folks?"

"Fine. They gave me money for rock candy. They're waitin' at the livery."

"I wondered what was in that sack. You better run along. Be a good boy, now."

"I will."

Tommy's scrambling run pounded against the boardwalk. Thad Jarrett's footsteps could no longer be heard.

CHAPTER TWENTY-SIX

The next day's edition of the *Travis Gazette* dominated the town of Travis. Rance, Stacey and Bo Jefferson spent much of the Monday before the election telling quizzical citizens they had nothing to add to what was in the newspaper.

The evening found the three men huddled in the sheriff's office, going over the night and overnight rounds. Bo was given the first opportunity to fend off questions while grabbing supper at Jerry's Restaurant.

Jefferson was whimsical as he pulled a telegram from his coat pocket before heading out for food. "I think Riley will be selling a lot of newspapers for many months. There may be some big stories coming out of Travis, Arizona. Maybe Riley will get national attention after all."

Rance eyed the telegram. "What do you mean?"

Bo handed the paper to Rance. "Read for yourself. The authorities are very interested in Kain Arnell. They've been keeping a close eye on Kain and suspect he may have done some underhanded work for the Conrad Western Railroad. Two U.S. Marshalls will be arriving later in the week to question him."

Dehner's eyes went over the telegram carefully. "Reading between the lines, I suspect the law is after Bradford Conrad, the president of the railroad. They are hoping Arnell will testify against his boss to save himself from a rope."

Stacey Hooper beamed. "Let us wish the authorities great success in their endeavors."

Anticipation was far ahead of the sunrise on voting day in Travis, Arizona. The restaurant and stores were opening early, preparing for the stream of people who would be coming into town to vote.

After having breakfast at Jerry's Restaurant, which began to serve while the sky was still a dark gray, Rance and Stacey headed for the sheriff's office. They met Bo Jefferson coming from the opposite direction. All three men noted the kerosene yellow which glared from the office window.

Bo nodded a good morning, then spoke in a soft but concerned voice. "Thad is already here. He relieved me about three hours ago."

"Thad shouldn't be on duty today—"

To Dehner's surprise, Jefferson cut him off. "No. On duty is exactly where Thad Jarrett belongs." The pastor paused, then continued. "Duty has always been important to Thad and now it's all he has."

The sheriff was sitting at his desk examining papers. He looked up and attempted a smile. "Good morning, gents." Jarrett's face was clean shaven but pale. His eyes were bloodshot and Dehner could read nothing in them.

Jarrett's chair made a familiar scraping sound as the sheriff stood up. "Rance, I would never have asked you here if I'd known you'd be tossed into Hell's deepest pit. Stacey, like I said yesterday, I'm sure happy you tagged along."

"Thad, we—"

Jarrett kept speaking as if Rance had said nothing. "Bo and I will be spending most of our day making sure there's nothing underhanded 'bout the voting, then monitoring the vote count. I'm obliged to you two for staying in Travis one more day to keep the lid on all the hoorawing that'll be going on."

Dehner tugged on his ear. "Stacey and I planned to hang around Travis for another week or so until you could find and train a deputy."

Jarrett's reply was curt. "Obliged, but Bo can help me out 'til then. You two gents need to get back riding your usual trails."

The lawman stopped speaking and looked around the office as if trying to comprehend what the usual trail was for him. When he spoke again it was in a clipped, businesslike manner. "Bo and I need to get over to the town hall. Rance, Stacey, thanks again."

Rance Dehner and Stacey Hooper accompanied the two men out of the office and watched them as they headed for the town hall.

Dehner spoke in a solemn voice. "Travis, Arizona is home for Thad Jarrett and Bo Jefferson. They have nurtured the town like it was a child. This is an important day in the town's history, and they are going to ensure that everything is done fair and above board."

Rance and Stacey watched until the sheriff and pastor vanished into the town hall, carrying out their duty.

Center Point Large Print
600 Brooks Road / PO Box 1
Thorndike, ME 04986-0001 USA

(207) 568-3717

US & Canada:
1 800 929-9108
www.centerpointlargeprint.com